Coveted
Passion
Sexy
Stories
Collection

VOLUME 24

10 EROTIC SHORT STORIES

ETHEN SHEAR

Publisher's Note: This is a work of fiction. Names,
characters, places, and incidents are a product of
the author's imagination. Locales and public
names are sometimes used for atmospheric
purposes. Any resemblance to actual people, living
or dead, or to businesses, companies, events,
institutions, or locales is completely coincidental.

Coveted Passion/ Ethen Shear. -- 1st ed.
Xplicit Press, an imprint of TLM Media LLC

ISBN-13: 978-1-62327-555-6
ISBN-10: 1-62327-555-5
eISBN: 978-1-62327-605-8

Printed in the United States of America

CONTENTS

1 THE MAID

Big, Black, and Made of Rubber

I'm Angie, a 22-year-old blond girl who studies architecture and, since the last month, I love to be tied up and used like a slave. Here's how it happened.

Since I'm studying architecture, most of my income goes to books and office supplies. It's hard living alone in a studio apartment. The rent is too high, and on top of that, I misplaced my vibrator, which was the only thing that's entered my pussy since I moved to New York. Living here is expensive, and I decided to take a part-time job as a maid for one of the house-cleaning companies in town. My first task was to clean the apartment of a high-street broker who was living in a building full of rich people. After a 40-

minute ride in a cab, I arrived at the address, only to see that no one was home. When I wanted to leave, the doorman stopped me and asked if I was the cleaning lady. Then, he gave me the key from the apartment and told me that Mr. Bruce, the owner, had to be at a meeting in LA. So he just left for the airport.

The apartment was stylish and huge. So huge, I was afraid to start cleaning. I decided to do what every other curious young woman would do, search the place. He had a nice home, expensive furniture, old scotch, and very fine suits. Yet, from the many things that he had, I was attracted by a big, metallic chest, locked with a letter lock. I thought, "What the hell," and entered the first code that crossed my mind: 6969. Surprised by my guess, I opened it, only to find some very interesting things: black leather masks and latex clothes, handcuffs, a mouth gag, many ropes, and finally, a big black dildo. "No! I won't. I mean, I shouldn't..." This was the only thing that I kept repeating in my head, while I just stood there with the big rubber dick in my hand. "But, I'm so horny! I haven't been fucked since two months ago," and I couldn't resist anymore. The next thing I know, the toy was halfway down my throat. I sucked it like it was the only dick in the world. Once

I realized what I've done, it was too late. My nipples were hard, my palms were sweaty, and my little pink pussy was wetter than a tropical rain. "If I'm gonna do this, I'm gonna do it right." Then, I started to put together a hot outfit, from the chest. When I was equipped, like a fuck pig, I went to the bed and tossed myself on it. Only then, I saw that on the ceiling was a huge mirror right over the bed, like in the VIP rooms from the whorehouses. I could see me. I was so hot I almost had an orgasm only from watching myself. Wearing just a pair of black high-heeled boots and a black mask, with a dildo in hand, licking it and sliding it on my nips, I was ready to start enjoying the pleasure of something that could go so deep inside me and make me scream, like I was fucked for the first time. So, I jammed it in my pussy and it felt wonderful. Nothing else mattered, in that moment, and, because of the pleasure, I grabbed one of my boobs and squished it so hard, my nails left a deep mark inside them. I could feel the pain, but I wouldn't stop. I liked what was happening to me and I didn't even notice that someone entered the house.

Caught in the Act

It was Bruce, the owner. His flight was delayed and he returned home. I saw him watching me, and I remained speechless, and scared. He was shocked and confused. We just stood there, without saying anything, for at least two minutes. Then, finally, he said, "What the fuck is happening? Who the fuck are you, whore... The fuck is this?"

"I... I... I clean. Sorry mister!"

"Well bitch, you were supposed to clean the house, not fuck yourself on my bed. You're so gonna lose your job for this!"

"No mister! Please! I'll do anything I swear!"

"Well, since you're so horny little slut, I got the right thing for you!"

I was so scared when he took off his shirt. I thought he was going to make me suck his cock, but it wasn't that simple. He went to the chest and brought back a pair of handcuffs and 12 feet of rope. Then, he tied the rope to a hook on the ceiling, handcuffed my hands, grabbed me by my hair, and put me on my knees in the middle of the room. After my cuffed hands were tied with the rope, he pulled it, just to put me in a position ideal for a mouth fuck. I was on my knees with my hands cuffed, over my head.

"Ok bitch, now, let's talk! What's your

name?"

"I'm Angie, sir!"

"From now on, you will address me as master. Understood cunt?"

"Yes."

"Yes what, slut?"

"Yes, master!"

I was so scared, I couldn't even scream for help. The only thing I could do was look at his shoes, because I was too afraid to look him in the eyes.

"I see you like my shoes! Well, if you like them so much, maybe, you should lick them." Then, he raised the left foot slowly, touching my boobs on his way up, to my mouth.

"I said, lick my shoe, you miserable slut." So, I licked his shoe. It tasted horrible, and I almost puked.

"That's right, bitch. That's your place, now. From now on, you shall be my slave. Say it!"

"I shall be your slave, master!"

"Good slave. For that, you will get a prize. Look up and open your mouth, like a good slave."

With fear taking over my mind, I decided to play his game and, maybe, I'll escape from there alive. I looked up at him. On his face I could read only pleasure; cold, heartless pleasure. After I opened my mouth, he spit in it. I have to admit, I've wanted somebody to spit on me while having sex since I was a horny teen.

"Do you want to feel a cock in your mouth, slave?"

"Yes, master!"

"Say it!"

"I want to feel a cock in my mouth!"

"And, you will, sex slave!"

He took out his cock. It was a beautiful one, about 8 inches, circumcised, and thick. I opened my mouth so fast, like I wanted his cock down my throat as soon as possible. He told me to lick it. So, I did it. After a while, I realized that I was sloppy. I saw the saliva dropping on the floor from his cock. I think he liked that, because he didn't scream at me again. Then, he grabbed my hair and shoved the long dick down my throat. He pushed the cock so hard in my mouth; I began to gag on it. He took down my mask to see my face, which was covered in mascara tears. As if it wasn't enough, he spit on me, again. My face looked awful, but at the same time, it was the kinkiest and slutty look that I ever had. Not even the slutty cat costume from Halloween could give me such a kinky look. I truly began to like it and I felt horny again. Suddenly, he stopped fucking my mouth and told me to open my mouth. That was it! He came into my mouth.

"Swallow, slut! I want you to swallow my cum." I obeyed what he said and I swallowed.

"How's the taste of cum, slave?"

"It tasted delicious, master. The best cum I've ever swallowed! I wish you could give me more."

"Next time, slave. Next time."

"What do you mean, next time?"

Settling the Deal

He uncuffed me and I fell on my hands, right on the saliva, from the floor. I was confused. So, I repeated my question.

"What do you mean, next time?"

"Well, from now on, I'd like you to be my personal slave. Of course, I'll make your time worth it."

He reached for his pants and gave me $650. It was wonderful. I could finally pay my bills and treat myself to a nice dinner in a fancy restaurant. He was another man, calm and relaxed. The mean attitude and strong language disappeared. Yet, I was still horny, and since he wasn't a real danger and everything was just a game, I offered him a bonus.

"Here's the thing... How would you like to take turns, and be my slave, now?"

"No, no, no! I don't want to be rude, or anything, but I'm too tired and I think my dick won't get up again today."

"I wasn't talking about your dick."

So, I grabbed the handcuffs and tied his hands to the bed. He was even more surprised than I was when he caught me.

"What the fuck are you doing, now? Are you a crazy nympho or something?"

"You're not the only one that wants to cum, baby."

I couldn't believe that I was doing that. I jumped on him, in the reverse cowgirl position, and put my wet pussy on his mouth. Then, I began to move my hips, and he started to lick the hell out of my pussy. I liked that so much, and I screamed so hard that the whole city of New York could hear that I'm having an orgasm.

"Squirt in my mouth, Angie! Please, squirt in my mouth! I want to feel your tight pussy juice on my face."

So much time had passed since I had an orgasm that powerful and intense. I squirted so much that the whole bed was a wet mess. After my arms stopped shaking, I turned and I started to lick my own juice from his face. I've swallowed cum, and I licked pussies before, but I never tasted my own squirt. It has such a good taste and I could see that Bruce liked that kinky move, too.

After we calmed down, he told me to bring him a cigar and a glass of whiskey, from the living room. There, I saw a picture of him and a young Asian lady, dressed up in dominatrix suits.

"Here are your things! Now, what's the deal with the other lady?"

"Oh! You saw the picture. That's my wife. Don't worry, you will meet her."

"What do you mean by, 'you will meet her'? Does she know about us, already?"

"We have an open marriage, and you are not the first one that was tied in my bedroom. But, that's enough questions for now. Give me your number and I shall call you when I need you, since I'm your master and you are my slave."

So, I gave him my number and left his apartment. I was a little ashamed. Becoming a slut is not too easy for me. I never accepted money for sex before. This was difficult. On the other hand, being a slave might be the right job for me and, to be honest, I liked being used.

Meeting the Lady

Two weeks had passed since my first experience in the slave business, and I kind of missed those moments. I was getting hornier and the phone didn't ring. To get the stress out, I tried to masturbate, but a banana was nothing compared to my master's lips on my clit. Finally, I received a text message. "Meet me at the apartment in 2 hours. Don't be late, slave." That was a relief. I could only hope that my pussy would get a real cock this time.

I arrived at the place and found a note on the door, which said, "Get naked and crawl into the bedroom," and that's what I did. Yet, in the bedroom, there was no Bruce. It was just the Asian lady lying on the bed, with her legs spread and a whip in her hand.

"Hello slave! I'm Xin Ling and this is my pussy. Eat it!"

Well, that was unexpected, but I did what I was told, like the good slave that I am. I crawled upon the bed and begin to lick, suck, and eat that little Asian pussy of my master's wife. She turned, and I understood that it was time to lick her ass. I wasn't too happy about it, because I'd never done such a thing. Yet, I did it. It wasn't too bad and she began to enjoy the kinky thing that I was doing.

"Turn around!" she said. "Spread your butt cheeks and don't scream."

Sitting there, with my eyes closed, I didn't know what would come. Then, I felt something wet on my asshole, like lube.

"Don't forget to shut up. If you scream, you'll regret it."

The next thing she did was put the whip handle in my ass. It was so painful that I burst into tears, but I didn't make a sound. She then took her phone and called someone.

"We are ready for you. Come in!"

After she hung up, I heard the door, and a voice telling me to prepare myself for some serious business. It was Bruce. He entered the room and kissed his wife. Then, he grabbed me by the hair and looked me in the eyes.

"Hello Angie! Are you ready to have your ass and pussy destroyed, today?"

"Please, be gentle, master!" I was a little scared. Off course, I wanted to be fucked, but not like that.

"Someone is afraid. Xin, please gag her. I don't want her screams to spoil our fun!"

"Ok, hun! Do you want me to tie her up, as well?"

"Hmmm! Maybe, we should get the bench, too."

"The bench? What the fuck is that?" I asked myself. Xin got some rope and tied my hands behind my back, while Bruce entered the room with a metallic, black leather bench. Xing slapped me and spit on me. Then, she told me to lie on the bench, facing downwards. She tied my legs and Bruce took the whip out of my ass and whipped me with it, on my entire body, until my whole skin turned red. Without any warning, he took his dick out of his pants and shoved it into my ass. The pain was so powerful and I screamed, so hard, like I wasn't even gagged. Without even caring, he continued to fuck me and slap me. I hardly turned my head to see if his wife was happy about this. She looked like she enjoyed it. In fact, she saw me looking at her and said, "Do you want to be un-gagged, slave?"

I nodded. So, she took the gag out of my mouth and put her foot in front of me.

"Suck my toe, slave!"

"Ok, Miss Xin."

"Hun, don't you want to let our slave pleasure you with her mouth?"

"Of course, dear! Go get your strap on."

Within the next minute, I had a dick in my mouth and a strap on in my ass. Xin fucked me harder than any man I know. She was so wild, and so aggressive, that she made me cry. When Bruce saw me crying, he stopped fucking my mouth and begin speaking to Xin. "Honey, stop it! You're too rough on her!"

"What do you mean, Bruce? She is a slave. I don't care about how rough I am on her!"

"Well, she is our slave and I care. Maybe, we should fuck her pussy, too!"

"For a moment there, baby, I thought you really cared about her. Ok, let's do it!"

Finally, it was the time for my pussy to be plowed. They untied me and tossed me on the bed. Bruce lay beside me and told me to jump on his cock. I knew what I had to do. I took his strong dick in my hand, and gently put it in my vagina. Then, Xin came from behind and shoved her strap on in my ass, again. They started to fuck me, slap me, and spit on me. I thought it would never end. After five minutes or so, I began to enjoy it too, but my feet were asleep and my ass was killing me. My pussy found the strength to squirt a little. When I felt that, I let myself get carried away and I didn't fight the pain. I learned, then, to use that pain to my advantage. I learned to enjoy the pain and that's how my well-fucked pussy was able to offer me the best orgasms that I ever had. When they got bored by this position, Xin told Bruce that she wanted a little cock for herself, too. So, she jumped on the bed and Bruce began to fuck her. Sitting alone, beside them, I could only watch a good anal sex show and, in the next moment, I had my hand down my pussy and two fingers inside. With a voice full of pleasure, Xin told me, "I heard your squirt tastes delicious, slave! I want to taste that, too. Come in front of me."

Sitting there, with Xing eating my pussy and my master fucking her ass, I couldn't think of anything else besides the fact that this job was the best job that I could ever have. I began to squirt on Xin's face, in her mouth. Judging after the fact that Bruce had a joyful look on his face, I knew that he had an orgasm, too.

"Come here, little slave." He told me. "See my wife's ass. I want you to suck every little drop of cum out of her ass!"

I couldn't wait for that to happen. Last time we met, he gave me his tasty cum, and I couldn't wait to taste it again. I licked and sucked Xin's ass. Then, she turned around and told me not to swallow. She began to kiss me and Bruce's cum was dripping down, from our mouths. He got a camera and took some pictures of us kissing and licking his sperm from each other's faces. After all was done, I got dressed and Bruce gave me $1000, Xin kissed me goodbye, and I went home.

Since then, every single week, I go to their place and have a beautiful time, just the three of us. My new job is to be a slave and I like it, very much.

2 DUNGEONS AND ORGASMS

Tanya

One night, when my roommate was asleep and I wasn't sleepy at all, I decided to take advantage of being alone and have a little "me" time. So, I lit up some candles and chilled on the couch with a good book. I just couldn't find anything interesting in my bookshelf. I searched for something worth reading in my roommate's school bag. That's how I found a book about sexual psychology and fetishes. Since nothing was worth reading, I thought that would have to do. I read about gays and lesbians, anal and oral sex, threesomes and orgies. But the subject that attracted me the most was a chapter about BDSM. In fact, it was so well written and so intense that I began to feel horny.

I could feel my nips getting harder and I couldn't stop moving my legs and my hips. While I was reading about a blonde girl forced to lick the ass of a dominatrix, my heart was beating harder and harder, until I realized that I was touching my boobs. I kept reading and, with my right hand going lower and lower, I couldn't concentrate enough to hear that my roommate woke up and saw me. She was watching how I began to unbutton my jeans and how I slipped my hand into my pink panties. She didn't move at all, and I continued to masturbate, slowly and passionately. My panties were getting wetter and I only stopped when I had an orgasm. I dropped the book on the floor, leaned my head back, and let out the sound of pure pleasure.

After getting myself together, I rose from the couch and saw my roommate, Tanya. She had long, red hair and black eyes, wearing just a pair of shorts and covering her huge boobs with her hands. I was sexually attracted to her from the moment she moved in. Seeing her getting out of the shower naked and sleeping topless made my secret desires get stronger. Some nights I just wanted to start kissing her whole body and make passionate love to her. I couldn't resist any longer and I made a move on her, right then. We started kissing and I had my hands all over her perfect body, but she stopped me and said, "Not now, Susie. You need something more than fooling around with your roommate. Your passion and desires are too wild to be tamed with some occasional girl-on-girl sex."

"What do you mean, Tanya? You don't like me? I'm such a fool. How could I think that you were willing to do me? I'm so ashamed."

"Hey, don't be. I like you, very much, and I'd totally do you in ways you couldn't even imagine, but you need something else right now."

I didn't know what she was talking about. Was it just to make me feel better for rejecting me, or did she know something that I didn't? With a trembling voice I asked her, "What do you mean, 'something else'? Something else, like what? A man, or a gangbang, or what?"

"Something more."

"More than a gangbang? Like a horse, or something?"

"Don't be silly, Susie! I'll arrange for something. I'll give you a phone number. Call that number tomorrow morning, and they will give you additional details. Tell them that you have a recommendation from Tanya. They know what that means. Now, get back on the couch and close your eyes!"

She tossed me on the couch and undressed me. Without even kissing me, she placed her hand on my pussy. That felt awesome and I didn't want it to stop. She slowly massaged my clit and, with the other hand fingered my pussy. With my eyes closed, I could only imagine what that looked like. She needed just two minutes to give me a powerful orgasm, which made me cum all over her magical hands. I came a lot because I could hear how the squirt was dripping on the floor. She touched my lips with her wet fingers and without even thinking, I licked and sucked her long fingers covered in my own pussy juice. It tasted delicious, like pure pleasure. After giving me one of the best orgasms of my life, she just kissed my pussy once and told me to go to sleep because tomorrow would be a big day for me. I wanted to ask her more questions, but she went to her room and I was too carried away from the pleasure to follow her. So, I just fell asleep.

The House of Pleasure

When I woke up, it was a beautiful Friday morning, and the sun was shining all over my naked body. I couldn't remember very much from last night.

Actually, I thought that I was dreaming, but when I wanted to get up I felt something wet on the floor. It was the thing that reminded me that Tanya made me cum like one of the actresses from the "squirt bukkake" porn I use to watch when I wanted to masturbate. "So, it was real. I didn't dream. I wonder what she is doing now."

I went to her room, to check up on her and to ask her some questions, but she wasn't there. Instead, on the bed, I found a note with a phone number and a reminder: "Don't forget to mention my name."

After a few hours of wondering about what the hell happened last night and analyzing the situation, trying to guess who I might call, I decided to just do that. There's no way to guess.

A man's voice said, "How did you get this number?"

"Hello, mister!"

"I asked, 'How did you get this number'?"

"Come on, Susie! Pull yourself together! The man asked a question, answer him." I thought.

"Tanya gave it to me."

"Right, Tanya! Are you a friend of hers?"

"I live with her, mister. She is my roommate."

"Do you want our services?"

I didn't know what the hell he was talking about? "What services?" I thought. Maybe, it has something to do with Tanya's job. She was missing a lot for her job. Ok, I'll play her game. What can I lose?

"Yes mister, I would love your services."

"Ok, you will need to be free all day. Get a car, or a cab, and come to the address that will be texted to you. Be here in three hours. Don't bring any luggage. See you here."

Then he hung up. I was afraid, but I trusted Tanya. She was a real woman. Nothing could touch her. She was tough, but she kept her feminine side, which made her have a super hot attitude. I left home, without any luggage, and after a one-hour drive in a cab, I arrived at the destination. It was a little neighborhood, near a lake, and the house where I was told to be was the biggest one there.

As I entered the front door, I became worried. I saw that in the house was nothing but a man with a leather mask and black pants. I was in shock.

"What the hell is this?" I asked, scared and with a very loud voice. The door slammed behind me and made me scream so loud, but the man with the mask wasn't even concerned about anyone hearing that.

"Welcome to the 'House of Pleasure'!

You can scream louder if you want. No one will hear you, here. Miss Pain, please prepare our guest for why she came here!"

From across the big room, a door slowly opened, and I could just see a tall woman with high-heeled boots and latex gloves. Her big boobs looked squished by a leather vest she was wearing and the pants had holes in them, which would allow her pussy and ass to be fucked without getting naked. In her left hand, she carried a long whip, which she was playing with; licking it and sliding the handle on her clitoris, while she slowly came towards me. She had a red ponytail, exiting trough her latex mask, and once she arrived in front of me she bitch slapped my face. That's how I recognized that Miss Pain was, in fact, Tanya.

"Tanya, what the fuck is happening here? What is all this about?"

"I'm not Tanya for you, bitch. Here, you will address me as Miss Pain."

"What? Tanya, what's going on?"

"I said, Miss Pain, bitch!"

Then she whipped my boobs, not too hard, but enough for me to understand the fact that she was the dominatrix there and I was about to be dominated. Just like the story from her book, the story that made me so horny.

I decided to play her game. She ripped my shirt and my bra off. I remained topless. Then, the scary man came in front of me and started to feel my round boobs. He slapped them like I was being punished for having such amazing round boobs. Then, he pinched my nipples, and from his pocket, he took two metallic clips and linked them with a chain. He put them on my nipples, and by the chain, he dragged me across the room where a steel pole was hanging horizontally from the roof, and where Miss Pain cuffed my hands. I was sitting in a very unpleasant position, with my hands cuffed by the pole, and I was nearly touching the ground. That man cut my jeans off of me with a big knife, and Miss Pain pulled my panties until the front string had entered my pussy, giving me a powerful burning feeling.

"Her panties are wet. That means she enjoyed it."

I didn't know I wet my panties. I didn't know I liked what was happening to me, but it appeared that my pussy loved it. The man told me to suck his middle finger and, when it was wet enough, he spread my butt cheeks and put his thick finger in my ass.

"You have a very tight asshole, slut! Don't worry, when you leave this place, you will be able to put a grapefruit up your ass."

Miss Pain whipped me and slapped me

for about ten minutes. She even played with my clitoris, rubbing it with the tip of her leather boots. I didn't know what to think. There was a lot of pain in this game, but on the other hand, I liked it and I didn't want her to stop. Miss Pain uncuffed me and dragged me by the chain down some stairs, where a big metallic door was standing between me and some scary vibrating noises.

The Dungeon

When the man opened the door, I could see a big dungeon with a lot of weird contraptions in it like the ones used in BDSM porn. They tossed me there and told me to prepare myself for a night full of pain and hardcore sex. After they shut the door, I began to look around the dungeon. That's when I saw a black girl on a wooden bed. Her hands and feet were strapped to the bed. She had some sort of dildo in her pussy and anal beads in her ass. On her nipples she had some clips, just like mine, and her mouth was gagged. She seemed asleep. I went closer to her and I saw that her face and hair was covered in cum. Her whole body was filled with whip marks. When I wanted to look closer at her pussy, she woke up and looked at me. I understood from her eyes that she wanted to be ungagged. So, I did that.

"I'm Shareen! Please, play with me!"

"What?"

"Uncuff me and let's play with our pussies!"

"Are you crazy? What if they come and see us? Do you want to be punished?"

"I would love to, that's why I'm here. Why the fuck are you here if you don't want to be punished?'

"My friend told me to come here!"

"And... Don't you like what they are doing to you?"

"Well, I don't know. I guess I like it."

"That's a good girl. Now uncuff me and let's play something. The keys are under the bed."

I took the key and I released her hands and feet. Shareen took the clips down, from my nips, and started to lick them. I felt so good and so scared at the same time, so I stopped her. I got her off me, and with my mouth, I took the anal beads out of her ass and dropped them on the floor. With the dildo from her pussy, I began to fuck her ass, while eating her pink pussy. I played with my tongue on her clitoris, until she came in my mouth and all over my face. Just when she finished her orgasm, Miss Pain entered the room and saw my face covered in Shareen's juice.

"Oh, I see you made a new friend. You

only knew her for 20 minutes and you let her already cum in your mouth. That means you are a slut, Susie. And, what does a slut deserve?"

"Punishment?"

"That's right. Punishment. And, since you love the taste of squirt so much, I have the perfect punishment for you. Come with me, slut!"

"Yes, Miss Pain!"

I was put on a bed and cuffed. The bed turned me upside down and bent at 90 degrees. It nearly brought my pussy near my mouth. She took out an electric vibrator from a bag, and placed it on my clitoris. The vibrations were so powerful and the feeling was so strong that my pussy began to contract, harder and harder. Soon, it became so tight that she could only insert two fingers in me. Her foot was on my neck. Breathing became a hard thing to do. Soon, I squirted all over my face and body. The asphyxia only made the orgasm stronger and the sound of my voice made Shareen wish she were there on the bed, in my place.

After hearing my voice, the masked man entered into the dungeon and took me down from the bed. I was tossed in the other corner of the room, where a bunch of ropes were tied to a strange contraption. In five minutes, or so, I was tied up and hung by the roof. My body was suspended in the air, just at the right height from the ground, which could easily allow someone to fuck me. I was facing downwards and couldn't see anything happening around me. The only thing that I saw was a big purple, rubber strap on, which was worn by Tanya. She started to slap me on the face with it and they commanded Shareen to whip my tits, until I was crying. In the next moment, without any warning or lube, just with a spit between my butt cheeks, the masked man put his thick dick in my ass and he fucked me harder than I've been fucked in my life. I started to cry, but I didn't want them to stop, and they didn't. I think I screamed too much because Miss Pain grabbed me by the hair and told me to open my mouth, just to put her huge strap on down my throat. In that moment, I was whipped my another slave. I was gagging and leaving my drool on a dildo, and my little pink asshole was destroyed by a man who's name I didn't even known.

The masked man stopped from violently fucking my anus and Miss Pain took her rubber dick out of my throat. I was happy to be able to breathe normally, and when I opened my eyes, I saw a big splash of my drool on the floor. She took Shareen by the hair and, literally, cleaned the floor with her ebony face. Then, Miss Pain placed Shareen under me and told her to look directly in my eyes. The masked man returned, with a long stick that had a metallic, pointy head and made weird electrical noises. I could just watch Shareen's face, covered in my saliva, which I thought was gross and hot, at the same time. I even wanted to lick it. When the masked man touched her pussy with the electric stick, she screamed louder than me when I was getting my ass ruined. Then, she crawled right into the other corner of the room, crying.

After that, I knew it was my turn, and when feeling the electric shocks on my beautiful tight pussy made me cry as well, the masked man wouldn't stop. I couldn't take it anymore. The lower part of my body fell asleep. I couldn't feel my legs and the skin from my vagina burned, like the fires of hell. I screamed for help and begged them to stop. Eventually, after seven or eight shocks like that, they finally stopped. I was taken down from the ropes, untied, and left on the floor. Miss Pain ordered Shareen to lick my pussy, while she was getting fucked by the masked man, right in front of me.

When the sex scene was almost finished, he came in front of us and told us to open our mouths for a treat. I couldn't wait for this. Believe it or not, swapping and swallowing a stranger's sperm was the only normal thing that could happen to me that day. But Miss Pain took that away from me, too. She told him to turn around and we were ordered to lick his asshole, while she was performing the greatest sloppy blowjob. One that was so great, I could only dream of doing something like that to a man's dick. When he was ready to cum, she jerked him off, until he came on the floor. I guessed we were supposed to lick it off, and I was right. It had such a good taste, even if it was from a floor, filled with saliva and pussy juice. It felt right, like the ending of a wild sex dream.

After all was finished, they just left us there and left the dungeon. After 20 minutes, Tanya came back with two trench coats, for me and Shareen, and took us upstairs to clean ourselves. Taking a shower was such a pleasant feeling, after a day of orgasms and pain. When the time had come for us to leave, I kissed Shareen and got in Tanya's car. On the way home, she explained to me what just happened. I found out that she was one of the best dominatrix in the country. Many VIPs entered her dungeon. Shareen was the wife of a powerful governor and she paid $3000 for her services. That was something unexpected about my hot roommate. She told me that it would be lovely to teach me all the secrets of this job. The next six months were filled with hardcore training and passionate sex. It was the best period of my life. In a short time, I learned all she could teach me and I became a real dominatrix. My name, from now on, is Miss Scream!

3 MY FIRST MAN

Some Kind Of Party

It was a summer night in my town, and I stormed out of the house after a huge fight with my girlfriend. She was upset that I didn't make more money. I'm a real estate agent, so I earn pretty decent money. Yet, she's a bitch, and bitches love money. As I was saying, I left my house, not planning to come back for at least ten hours. I was walking alone on the streets.

I remembered that my good friend, Greg, was having a party at his place. Since there was nothing to do, the party sounded just fine. I arrived there and was surprised to find only Greg and this blond girl, Anna. The rest of the party left earlier to a concert that was taking place in a pub nearby. Since there was no way I was going home that night, the only alternative was spending the night in a motel. There was no way I was doing that. We began to party, the three of us. Tequila shots and beers were flowing like rivers. We even did some body shots and it was awesome. Alcohol was the thing that left Anna topless and the party seemed to turn into a good old-fashioned threesome. With a bossy attitude, she demanded us to take off our pants. Then she started to suck our dicks. I was feeling good, but it didn't last too long because Anna, drunk as fuck, blacked out, leaving me and Greg horny.

"So what now! Should we fuck her like that, or should we stay horny all night?" asked Greg.

"I don't know, man! I think if we fuck her it will be considered rape, and I don't want to be a rapist."

"Well, Tony, you're right about that, but it doesn't change the fact that I'm hornier than a high school boy."

"I don't know what to say. Maybe, it's for the best, you know. I got a girlfriend waiting for me at home."

"That bitch? Screw her! I say let's continue the party. Just the two of us."

And out of the blue, he placed his hand on my cock. I didn't even know what to say or how to react.

"Don't worry! It will be fine. Trust me!"

How could he tell me to trust him? What was he doing? I didn't know he was gay, and I certainly knew I wasn't. Without even noticing, my cock liked Greg's big hand touching and stroking it because, in no time, it was fully erect. When Greg saw that, he just looked deep in my eyes and smiled. Slowly, he kneeled in front of me and shoveled my 8 inches of manhood down his throat. I was surprised to observe that he was doing a good job down there. So far, it was the best blowjob of my life. Not even once did his teeth touch my penis. I decided to let myself get carried away that night. So I stopped him and told him that we should go to his bedroom.

Greg's Bedroom

Climbing up the stairs to his bedroom, I could see him from behind. He had a great well-built body. All his contracted muscles made him look like one of the Greek gods. When we entered his bedroom, I thought that, maybe, it was time to take some action. So I pushed him on the bed and started playing with his dick while looking in his eyes. He liked it. It was showing on his face that he liked it, and when I put his cock in my mouth, he started moaning. I couldn't believe that I was sucking a man's penis. I was sucking the cock of one of my closest friends. That was the moment when I panicked and stopped.

"Hey! Why did you stop, Tony? What's wrong?"

"All... All of this is wrong. I have a girlfriend! I'm not gay. At least, I don't think so."

"Let me ask you something, Tony. Did you enjoy it so far? Be honest!"

"I don't know, man. I guess so."

"There's no such thing as gay or straight. What only matters is what makes you feel good, what you want, and if you have the courage to take it. Set yourself free from all the misconceptions and enjoy yourself!"

Those were the most accurate and clear words anyone had said to me about life. I wasn't scared anymore and I jumped on him. French kissing his pretty mouth and touching all of his body made me feel alive. I felt nothing but passion and arousal. He stopped me and, in the next moment, I was lying on the bed facing downwards. Then, Greg's lips started touching the back of my neck and he didn't stop there. He continued to kiss all of my body, making me feel like nothing else mattered right then. Honestly, I wanted him to kiss my virgin ass, too, but he already knew that and spread my butt cheeks apart. Then, with his soft tongue, he gently licked my pink ass. He told me to suck his middle finger, just to leave some saliva on it, so he could push it inside my ass. There was a little pain involved, but not much more that I could easily bear. After that, he spat on my ass and pushed his fully erect dick slowly inside me. That was painful for a couple of minutes. Then, I couldn't feel anything but pure pleasure—pleasure caused by my friend, Greg. But that wasn't all. After I was fucked well, he told me to sit in the doggy style position. I did what he said, and when he started to fuck me again, he grabbed my cock with his hand, too. While he was using my ass to pleasure himself, he didn't forget about me. I never experienced that feeling before—someone who cared so much about my pleasure. He was ready to have an orgasm. He started jerking me off and, in a short time, I came all over his bed and I could feel that he came inside me.

"Greg, that was awesome! I didn't think that kind of orgasm was even possible. How did you do that?"

"Well, Tony, it's not really a big deal. Once you lose all the inhibition, you'll do just fine."

"Well, it was fantastic. But unfortunately, I have to go home. I hope we can do this, again."

The Break-Up

It was 10AM when I arrived home, and my girlfriend, Jessica, was waiting for me, prepared for a fight. The argument lasted for three hours, and after a lot of screams and curses, I couldn't take it anymore.

"Get out of my house, bitch! And never come back! I'm sick of all your shit. I never want to see you again."

"Fine! If you want it, I'll go. But remember this. You'll never find someone like me."

"I hope so. Now, get lost. We are over."

Once she left the house, I called Greg. There was no one to call except him. After I told him what happened, he came at my house in no time. Once he entered the door, I jumped on him and started to rip off his clothes so aggressively that even I was surprised. There was no way of holding that in.

"Greg! I want you bad and I want you now. Right here, on the couch."

"Calm down, man! Are you sure you want this now?"

"Never been so sure about anything in my whole life. Now, shut up and suck my cock."

I know I told him to suck my cock, but that wasn't what happened. I grabbed his head and started to mouth-fuck him. I pushed my cock so deep down his throat I made him gag and his saliva was dripping all over the floor. When I realized that, I was done with his mouth. I turned him around and placed his hands on the wall. Without even warning him, I jammed my dick in his ass. Even though he was screaming in pain, I didn't stop. Fucking Greg like this felt great. Soon, he stopped screaming and asked me if we can go on the couch. I accepted. He lay on his back and I put his feet on my shoulders so I could fuck his ass properly. He was jerking off and I was fucking him. It was a great scene to see, especially after a disastrous morning like I had. I was looking in his eyes when he came all over his chest. When I saw that he came on his great body, I couldn't hold myself. I pulled my dick out and started licking his sperm and kissing him. After some more anal sex, I was ready to cum, too. He told me that he wanted my cum on his face. So I pulled out and started jerking until I came. With his eyes closed and his face covered in jizz, he began to suck my cock like he was hungry for every little drop of cum that could come out of it. After all was done, he cleaned himself and left, telling me that I needed some time to think. I didn't hear from him for a while. He wasn't home, nor was he at the pub from the neighborhood, and he always rejected my calls.

A Crazy Night

Two weeks had passed since I last saw Greg, and the feeling kept getting stronger. I jerked off a couple of times. I even tried to fuck my ass with a dildo that I found in my ex-girlfriend's closet, but it was nothing compared to a man's strong dick inside me. Since Greg was nowhere to be found, I decided that I had to try my luck with another man. So I went to this place I knew in the city. It was a gay bar. I'd never entered a gay bar before, so I didn't know how to blend in. All the men knew that I was almost a virgin and they avoided me, except one guy, a tall, brunette man with dark eyes and a cool mustache. He introduced himself as John and offered me a drink. We got along pretty well, and after a couple of hours of drinking and chatting, he asked me if I wanted to get out of there and move the party to his place. I was a little scared, but he was looking good and I needed a man like him. This was going to be my first one-night stand with a man.

We arrived at his place, a nice studio apartment with a lot of great decorations. He had some nice paintings and a bathroom with a hot tub. That was a cool thing, and I asked him if we could chill out in the hot tub. He liked the idea and, without even asking me, he stripped off all of his clothes. I could see a great, beautiful cock, big and thick. I couldn't resist, so I touched it.

"If you like it so much, why don't you give him a kiss, Tony?"

"I could give it more than a kiss, big boy."

I started to suck his big sausage while the bathtub was filling up. He turned me over and spread my legs, just to be able to lick my ass, and, at the same time, he was playing with my balls and cock. After the hot tub was filled up, we jumped in and started kissing. He put one finger in my butt. Soon enough, the second finger came too, then the third one. My ass was ready to be plowed. When he began to fuck me, the movements were so wild and the water was splashing all over the bathroom. His curly pubes were touching my ass, and that's how I knew that his big gun was completely inside me. I wished that it would never end, but he stopped and told me that it's my turn to pleasure him.

His butt was so hard and muscled up. The water that was covering all of his body made him look so hot. I couldn't believe that I hooked up with such a handsome man. I spread his ass and slowly pushed my meat inside him. It felt warm and pleasant. After all of my dick was inside him, he demanded me to fuck him as hardcore as I could. He was screaming and growling while my cock was entering his ass without any mercy. He told me to lean on the wall and close my eyes. I did that and I felt his tongue licking my cock, from the balls to the head. Then, he opened his mouth and pushed his head so hard I could feel my cock was going down his throat. He didn't even gag, not even once. He took my dick out of his mouth just to breathe. While jerking me, he told me to announce to him when I'm ready to cum. So I did, and just before I came, he pushed, once more, my dick in his mouth. I let all of my sperm go directly down his throat. He told me that he wanted to cum inside me. I bent over, waiting to be fucked, and after he had an orgasm, moaning and trembling, he put his mouth on my ass, waiting for the cum to come out. I noticed what he wanted. So I pushed the cum out of my ass to let him lick all the sperm that came out.

I enjoyed my one-night stand with John, and he asked to meet me again, but I couldn't think of anybody else but Greg. I felt guilty because I fucked another man and I wanted to share this with somebody. So I told everything to John. I was surprised to find out that John knew Greg. He even told me where I could find him. He was a bartender at another gay bar in town. So happy that I found out where he worked, I left John's apartment, took a taxi, and went to see Greg.

When he saw me, he didn't act surprised at all. It was as if he knew that I was coming.

"Did you make up your mind, Tony? Do you know what you want now?"

"I know what I want already! I want you, you stupid moron."

"I'm glad that you came to me. Are you sure you want this? It's not easy to have a relationship with a man."

"I don't care how hard it is. I just want to be with you. You are the only one who knows me and who cares about me. I want you to be mine. I love you."

When I said those words, he leaned over the counter and kissed me like I have never been kissed before. The entire bar saw what just happened and they started to applaud us. I never felt more alive. Greg's boss gave him permission to leave work, and we went to his place to celebrate our new relationship. That's the story of how Greg and I met. Now, after five years, we are still together, more happy than ever.

4 A WEEKEND IN L.A.

The Flight

My good friend Ken and I planned a trip to L.A. a long time ago. Yet, neither of us could find the time to do this because of the busy schedules we had for the last month. So, once we had a free weekend, it was time. We packed a few clothes and left for the airport. Once we got on the plane, there was nothing we could do except to wait for our landing at LAX.

The flight was boring and Ken fell asleep. I don't know if it was because of him sleeping or if he did it on purpose, but he put his hand on my crotch. I was stunned by this, but it was a pleasant feeling, I think, because my penis kept getting harder and harder. When it was fully erect, he grabbed it through my pants and started to squeeze it. When I looked at him, he seemed asleep. Then, I noticed a little smile on his face. I liked what he was doing to my cock, and I didn't stop him. When I saw the stewardess coming towards us, I moved his hand because I didn't want to have any problems with indecent public behavior. After she passed our seats, I rose up to go to the restroom, even if I didn't have to use it. I felt the urge to get away from Ken and clear my mind. Soon after, the door, which I left unlocked, opened, and Ken came in.

"Hello Charles! How is your flight?" he asked me, with a kinky tone in his voice. When I was questioning him about what the deal was with him touching my dick, he stopped me from talking by putting his finger on my mouth. Then, he kneeled in front of me, unzipped my pants, and took out my cook.

"Don't make a single noise. I'll give you something special," he said to me, but I didn't know what to do. If I stormed out of the restroom door, everyone could see that there were two men; if I screamed, it would be the same thing. Everybody saw that we were together, so it was possible to think we are a couple and we wanted to use the plane toilet for sex. So I stayed there, waiting for him to fulfill his wish of sucking my dick. I closed my eyes and hoped that it would be done soon. Then, a wet tongue started to lick gently the tip of my cock, and his hand was moving slowly, but firmly, up and down on it. In that moment, I let out a sound of pleasure.

"I knew you would like it. Now, keep your pretty mouth shut because I don't want to be caught blowing you." He looked at me when he said this and, maintaining eye contact, he began to suck my fully erect sausage as if it were made of gold. It was so intense and he was doing such a good job sucking it—and playing with my balls—that it didn't take me more than five minutes to reach an orgasm. I came so fast in his mouth that he was surprised. He smiled and showed me that he had a big load of cum in his mouth, which he played with a little. Then, he swallowed it.

He exited the restroom first and returned to his seat. I remained there a little while, thinking about the fact that Ken just gave me the best blowjob of my life. I didn't know what that meant and what I should do next. Should I return to New York once we landed, or should I stay with him and discuss this?

I didn't speak a single word to him throughout the rest of the flight, and he just kept smiling at me.

The Hotel Room

We landed at 11PM at LAX, and we took a cab to the hotel. There, I finally got the nerve to speak to him. When I asked him what the blowjob thing was about, he simply replied, "Don't act like you hated it! I know you liked it and you want some more."

"How can you know such a thing?" I told him with a trembling voice.

"Are you trying to say that if I get naked and jump on that bed, you won't even look at me?" He told me this while he was taking his clothes off. I started to sweat a little. I didn't know what to do. When he took his shirt down, my cock started to get bigger and harder. He saw that through my pants and he turned his back to me. When it was time for the pants to go off, he did it slowly, letting me see just a little piece of his sweet ass. When they fell off completely, I could see a big penis, thick and long, with no curves or imperfections. If I had to suck a man's dick, I'd want to suck this man's dick.

I approached him from behind, and when I had my hands all over his great body, he turned his head and we started kissing. It was wonderful; he was a great kisser. I gently put my hand on his fantastic cock, and the action began. While I was jerking him off with one hand, I used the other one to feel his strong ass. His butt cheeks felt like they were made of steel and I could hardly get my fingers between them. I gave him my middle finger to lick. After that, I pushed it hard into his tight ass. I did that just because of what he put me through on the plane. Yet, when I saw his face, I knew he liked it.

When his dick was fully erect, I made the next move. It was just like in that restroom, but this time I had his meat in my mouth and a finger in his ass, too. While blowing him, I could feel his ass contracting on my finger. He looked me in the eyes and told me to put two more fingers in him. His voice started to fill with pleasure and the only words he said were, "Suck it, Charlie! Suck it! Faster!!!"

When I thought that he was ready, I pushed him on the bed and he put his feet around my body. As I was looking him directly in his green eyes, I pushed my cock, slowly but firmly, into that little pink ass of his. He rolled his eyes and started moaning. I didn't know if my dick was too big, but when I entered it half in his ass, he stopped me.

"Push it, Charlie!" he said to me. So, I pushed it, as hard as I could. In that moment, he screamed, but it wasn't all pain. I could hear pleasure in his voice. "Now fuck me like a beast, Charlie! Fuck me hard!"

When I heard that, I knew that it was going to be a crazy night. He was screaming while I was pulling my sausage out of his ass. Then, I pushed it back in with all of my power. Every time my dick was fully inside of him, he would close his eyes and drag his nails through the skin of my back.

"Cum inside me, Charlie!" Those were the words I waited for. I kept myself so hard from cumming, and when I finally could do that, my body was no longer capable of doing anything. We were both finished. I just fell on him and he was as done as I was. I could feel his heart beating like a drum. We sat there naked, and we kissed a couple of times. Eventually, we fell asleep just like that.

The Shower

The next morning, when I was about to wake up, a lot of thoughts were going through my sleepy head. I was concerned that last night was a mistake. What if I blew off a beautiful friendship just for sex? I had to admit: that was one of the best sexual experiences that I ever had. But still, was it worth it? All those thoughts were gone when I opened my eyes and saw Ken looking at me, smiling.

"How long have you been awake?" I asked him.

"Just for an hour, or something like that," he said to me, like he spent just five minutes watching me. I was happy in that moment. All the stress and worries caused by my career were gone. And it was all because of Ken.

"Wake up and get dressed! We are going out," I told him with a demanding voice. He asked me, "Where?" But I didn't know how to answer.

"Well, we are in L.A. We could go everywhere."

I told him that the shower was awaiting me, and he asked me if he could come with me. I usually need to take the first shower of the day alone to plan my schedule, but what the hell! I was on vacation so we got in the shower together. I knew from the start that there was not going to be any washing in that shower. We let the water run down on our bodies. Then, he told me to turn around and put my hands on the wall. I couldn't see what he was doing, but I felt his teeth biting one of my butt cheeks. It felt great. He kissed and bit me. Then, when he got to my ass, he started licking it. His tongue on my hole was the thing that I needed to start a perfect day. Then, he started pushing one of his thumbs inside of me while licking and sucking my balls from behind. With the other hand, he was playing with my cock, and when it was hard like wood, he got up and hugged me from behind. While kissing my neck and biting my ear, he whispered to me, "Now, it's my turn to feel how tight your ass is!" That was the only warning I received from him before he took his meat in and penetrated my sweet ass with it. The feeling was great: a little pain at the start, but when he started moving back and forth, I could feel pleasure. It sure felt like he knew what he was doing. Meanwhile, he continued to jerk me off. The shower was dropping water on us, and the sun was shining through the bathroom window. It was perfect. I wanted more and I told him to be wilder. We were fucking like two drunken college boys who just discovered their sexuality. It was wonderful. I told him that I wanted to have our orgasms at the same time. I didn't even finish my sentence because I started cumming on the bathroom wall. I could feel his orgasm in my body. We were both trembling and moaning together. I turned towards him and we started kissing under the shower. It was the perfect Saturday morning in an awesome city like Los Angeles.

Under The Boardwalk

The day in the city was great. We skipped breakfast and took lunch at a fancy restaurant. We drank wine in the middle of the day, and we walked on the beach with our shoes off. When the night came, it was party time. Ken knew a fine club from the time he'd traveled a lot to L.A. for some meetings and work-related stuff. The atmosphere in that club was great, with lots of people having fun. There was good music and many drinks you could choose from.

We drank and danced for a couple of hours. Then, I met this girl, Jessica, an ex-coworker of mine. I had an adventure once with her, but that didn't spoil our friendship. We got along well. I danced with her a little. She told me that she was single and that she missed the times when we were colleagues, stuff like that. In a moment of weakness, caused by too much alcohol, she kissed me. Just like that, I couldn't see it coming. When Ken saw that, he just stormed out of the club and left me there with her. I didn't even try to explain to Jessica what happened because I was too concerned about Ken leaving. When I ran after him, he was nowhere.

I was desperate because I didn't want our time together to end, not so soon and not like that. Then, I remembered what he told me earlier that day when we were on the beach. While we were walking hand in hand at sunset, he showed me a boardwalk nearby the hotel in which we were staying. Under that boardwalk was a beautiful place where Ken used to go alone after a hard day of work while he was in town.

I ran as fast as I could and I only hoped that he was there. When I arrived, there was no sign of Ken. Then, I saw his clothes near the water. He was swimming. I got naked and jumped into the water. Once I was close to him, I started to explain everything. He told me that he believed me and that he felt sorry for disappearing like that. We kissed and hugged. Then, we spent a little more time in the ocean, skinny-dipping.

When we got out of the water, he took me by the hand and told me that he loved me ever since we first met. I didn't know what to say, and the only thing I could do was to kiss him. We were under the boardwalk, naked and kissing, while a lot of people were walking over the top of our heads, having no idea that we were there. We started making out and my hands were all over his body. Our cocks grew harder and they were rubbing one against another. I kneeled and started to suck his big cock. I jammed it down my throat and I didn't care that I was sloppy. He told me to lie on my back and he came over me in the 69 position. He was blowing me with so much passion that he had to stop a couple of times because I couldn't resist to cum in his sweet mouth. I licked his ass, and while I was sucking his dick, my two fingers were inside him. He turned over and took my cock in his hand. We were in the cowgirl position when he put the tip of my cock in his tight ass and started to move his hips back and forth. At the same time, he slowly let my cock make its way up his ass. As soon as he reached the spot he wanted, he started to literally jump on my cock. We were both moaning very loud, but it was okay because the noise made by the ocean's waves covered the sound of our pleasure.

Ken let himself all the way down on my cock and started to jerk off while moving a little, making me ready for an orgasm. He came all over my chest and a little on my face. Then, he rose and started to suck me until I came in his mouth. He swallowed my cum, but I think it wasn't enough for him because as soon as he was finished with my cock, he started to lick the sperm on my chest. It was so hot and kinky. I couldn't believe he was doing that, but I loved it. When he was almost ready, I kissed him and we swapped some of his cum. It was delicious.

After we were done, we just stood there, waiting for the sun to rise. While we were watching our first sunrise together on the beach of L.A., I could think about no one else, and nothing else mattered, in that moment. It was just me and my Ken!

5 THE HOUSEWIFE'S SECRET

Red Wine

One summer day, when my husband and kids had gone hiking and I was alone at home, one of my neighbors, Nicole, asked me if I could keep her company. She recently divorced that crappy man of hers and things weren't too bright in her life. With the thought of doing something good for another woman, and since her house was the next one on the left, I just put a white beach dress on and left the house.

Once I arrived at her place, I saw her depressed. Her red eyes told me that she cried, a lot, that morning. I'm not a shrink and dealing with these kinds of problems are not part of my qualities. Not knowing what to do to make her feel better, I just asked if she wanted some wine. So we started drinking and chatting. When the bottle was almost empty, we started to feel the alcohol kicking in, and because of that, I think, but I'm not sure, she spilled some wine on my white dress. She panicked and kept apologizing. I panicked, too, because that dress was one of my favorites. I took it off and asked her where the washing machine was. She told me it was in the first room, on the right. So I ran there, and she ran after me. Yet once I entered the door, I didn't see a washing machine, anywhere.

"What the fuck, Nicole! This is your bedroom. How am I suppose to wash my dress in your bedroom?"

"Well, Denise! We can do something else in the bedroom."

Just then, I realized that I was standing in front of her, half naked. I only had a pair of lace panties on me, with no bra. She was coming toward me, unbuttoning her shirt. I was backing off, scared, until the wall stopped me. She placed one of her hands on the wall and whispered something in my ear, with a kinky voice.

"I want you, Denise!"

When I realized what she had said, I just closed my eyes and hoped that she was fooling around. Yet it wasn't like that, because she started to kiss me on the neck, going up, until we were face to face. I couldn't see her, but I could feel her breath on my skin. The next thing I know, her lips were touching mine, her hands were all over my body, and her tongue was trying to get in my mouth. After one of her hands reached my butt, she squeezed it so hard, I wanted to scream. Once I opened my mouth, she French kissed me and I couldn't stop her. The kiss was so full of passion that I started to feel aroused.

Her hand was now on my belly, sliding down, under my panties. When her fingers touched my clitoris, I almost fainted. She was rubbing my pussy with such a great talent that my nips got harder and I started moaning. As my pussy was getting wetter, I couldn't believe that a woman was offering me such a great sexual pleasure. By the time I truly realized what was happening, it was too late to back off. My whole body wanted her, my pussy was contracting, and my palms were sweaty. She stopped doing what she was doing to me and took me by the hand, to get me to her bed.

"I'll give you something you wouldn't ever forget," she told me, with a sexy voice. That was it, the first lesbian experiment of my life. I'd never done such a thing, but I'll admit that usually, lesbian porn goes great when I'm masturbating alone on the living room couch.

Totally ready to do this, I grabbed her hand and said to her, "Please, make me cum like no one ever did." Then, we started kissing and her body was touching my hot skin. She pulled off my panties, while kissing me all over the place. As she got to the belly zone, her kisses felt like the touch of a Goddess. Soon, her mouth was near my wet pussy, and when her lips touched my clitoris, I closed my eyes and grabbed her by the hair. The way she sucked my clit was unbelievable and everything was perfect. So perfect that my own moaning made me hornier than I already was. Soon, she let her tongue in the game, licking my sweet, pink cunt. She was a little sloppy and I understood why. One of her fingers, I don't know which one and I don't even care, entered my vagina. That was the time when the first orgasm came. I didn't squirt this first time. When she started fingering me while licking my cunt, I couldn't hold it anymore. Without any warning, I came all over her face. She stopped, immediately, and I panicked. Seeing that I was concerned about the fact that I squirted on her, she told me, "Don't worry about that. I like the taste of your orgasm. Do you want to taste it, too?"

She looked me in the eyes, while her finger was still inside me and not moving at all.

"I asked you if you want to taste it!" She repeated, while her finger started moving inside me, again. When I felt that, I tried to reach her face, but it was impossible for me to do that, because the pleasure was too high. She came over me and I started to lick my squirt off of her beautiful face, while she was fingering me, faster and faster. She told me that she wanted more of my sweet pussy juice. So I decided to take some action, on my own. She layed on her back and I placed my pussy on her face. I began to rub my clit, while she was playing with my boobs, and when the time came, I closed my eyes and started screaming. That's how intense my orgasm was. When I finally stopped squirting, I looked down at her. She was licking her lips. All of her face and her brown hair were covered with the juice that came out of my cunt.

While I was enjoying the most intense sex adventure of my life, the doorbell rang. It was my husband. I remembered, I left a note for him on the fridge, before I left the house. I didn't know how to react. If it hadn't been for Nicole, I would have opened the door, naked. She gave me a top and a pair of shorts from her closet, and before I left, she kissed me without saying anything.

The Backyard

That night, I couldn't think of anything except Nicole, with her beautiful round tits and her soft skin. Only when I was thinking of her, I realized that I didn't see her pussy at all. She didn't have the chance to take off her jeans. I felt guilty. I was the only one to be licked and fingered. I left her horny, like that. However, there was nothing I could do now.

While in my bed next to my husband, trying to sleep, the thought of her was keeping me awake. Only the image of her pretty face in my mind was making me horny. I couldn't take it anymore. So I told my husband that I couldn't sleep and that I was going to take some air in the backyard. He couldn't care less. He was half asleep.

I went downstairs and I texted Nicole. I sent her a simple text like, which said, "Hey! What's up?" Like nothing happened that day. She texted me back, saying that she was thinking of me, while trying her new vibrator. That was the thing that turned me on and probably the reason for my next move.

"Meet me in the backyard of my house." This was the text I sent her. After only five minutes, she was there, dressed in a red night robe coming silently towards me. When I was sure that nobody saw her coming, the kissing began.

"I'm sorry that I left you like that. I want you to feel exactly what I felt when you did all those beautiful things to me," I said this to her, with a sense of regret in my voice.

There's a big swing in my backyard and that's where I put her. Ready to go down, I spread her legs. She was wearing nothing under the robe. In the moonlight, I saw her pussy, which was gorgeous. She was freshly shaven and she had a small, kinky piercing in her clit. When I first touched her pussy with my lips, I had a feeling of some sort of power. With my mouth, I was going to offer pure pleasure to a woman. She took my hand and started to suck on my middle finger. She did that to be sure that the sound of her moans would not wake my husband and kids up. I did my best, while she was getting wetter. The taste of horny cunt was awesome.

"Bite my clit, Denise!" This was what she told me, when she put her hand in my hair. I slowly bit it. She started to move my head around, while her clitoris was between my teeth. She did that for a minute or so, and soon she had an orgasm. The squirt that came out of her pussy wet my white T-shirt. My nipples were easy to be seen under the moonlight; such hard nipples. When she was done, she raised me up and we sat, together, on the swing. I was playing gently with her pussy while we were kissing. She had to leave, because I couldn't risk being found with her, but she promised me that this would be our secret, from now on.

A Great Saturday Night

After a week of thinking about Nicole's sweet pussy, I was finally home alone. My husband was out of town for a conference, and the kids were with my mother-in-law. I called on a Saturday afternoon and I told her to come spend the night at my place. She accepted, telling me that she would come prepared. I didn't know what she was talking about. With the thought of a wonderful night in my head, I started to prepare the house. I lit some candles and I put a sexy outfit on. High heels and a piece of red lingerie made me look like a porn star. She was finally at my door, dressed in just a trench coat. Once in the house, she took it down and I was quite surprised by what I saw. She was wearing an extremely sexy latex suit, but the most surprising thing for me to see was a rubber cock hanging between her legs.

"How would you like to suck it, my love?" That was what she said to me. I would have never guessed that she possessed such a sex tool and, frankly, I'd only seen them in porn. Yet, judging from what happened the first time, I trusted her that it would be ok. After I got on my knees, I started to suck on the strap-on, right in front of the door. We didn't have the patience to get upstairs in my bedroom. She began to face fuck me with that fake cock and things got a little hardcore. I was completely sloppy, letting drool fall all over the dildo. She took it from my mouth, just to slap my face with it. My makeup, which I put on, just for her, was destroyed and mascara tears started to flow.

When I was done blowing the strap-on, she started to French kiss me. Then, we went to the couch. I was on my knees, again, and she was licking my pussy, from behind, wild and aggressive. I felt her tongue trying to penetrate my cunt and her nose was touching my little, pink asshole. Soon after that, she was licking my ass, like it was the best lollipop on the planet. She started fingering me, but two of her fingers were in my pussy and another one was in my butt. From a small pocket of her trench coat, she took out a string of beads. When she pushed one up my ass, I understood what they really were. The fun began when her strap-on was inside of me. Slow but firm, she pushed that entire thing in my cunt and it wasn't small at all. It was like eight or nine inches, I think. When all of the blue cock was in me, she started to fuck me so hard. I was screaming from the top of my lungs. The strange thing was, I couldn't feel any pain, only pleasure. The pleasure got bigger when she started to pull the anal beads, one by one, out of my ass. When the last bead was out, I could feel that my tight, cute asshole got larger. I think it got so big that it was easy to put two fingers in it without touching the walls. She then spit in my ass, only to take the dildo from my pussy and place it in there. It was the second time that I had anal sex. The first time was with one guy in college. He came in there, and the strange part was that he licked his own sperm after that. I can't say that I didn't like that, but it was the first guy I saw who swallowed his own cum.

Anyhow, I was anally plowed in that moment. The pain showed up, but it wasn't an unbearable pain, it was more like a pleasant one. She fucked me like no one else fucked me. I had so many orgasms; the floor was all covered in squirt. I stopped her and tossed her on the couch. Then, I took down the strap-on from her, and I saw that the dildo was detachable. With the dildo in my hand, I began to perform the best oral sex I could on her pussy. From the reaction of her body, I must say that I was doing pretty well. She soon came, without any warning, just like I did last week. But I managed to catch a large amount of squirt in my mouth. I raised and spit the entire squirt in her face and mouth. When she swallowed it, I felt kinky and powerful. When I jammed the dildo into her, she told me to be rough. With crazy movements, I almost tore apart her vagina, but she didn't complain. In fact, a lot of orgasms were coming, one after another, and she squirted just as much as I did. Wanting to have an orgasm, together, we engaged in the 69 position and we were licking each other's cunts, while fingering our asses. We came, together. That was the most awesome moment of my sex life. We showered together afterward, and slept naked in each other's arms.

The next morning, when I woke up, I felt like it was a dream. Then, I saw her next to me and I knew it was real. Since then, every time we have the chance, we fuck our brains out. This is our little secret.

6 LOVE AND SECRETS

Good Looking MILF

I'm Ashley, a redheaded 22 year old who is not afraid of herself. Being young and always horny is a bit of a problem, especially when boys are such jerks. If I need someone to fuck, that doesn't mean that I'm a whore. So, I'm stuck with this stupid ass boyfriend of mine. As I said, sex is the thing that I need the most, and it's impossible to find a guy that can give me exactly what I want. So for two years now I've been bisexual. With women it is something else. They are caring when fucking. Usually I like to pick up girls in a lesbian bar near my workplace. It is a lot of fun and I'm there at least a couple of nights every week. This is how I met Tasha, a great MILF from Hurricane. She had a very sexy accent and big round boobs. A delicious ass was covered by her short skirt and she was wearing high heels. I was stunned when she approached me. The only scenario that I could think of was me between her long legs, licking her cunt.

"Hi baby! Want some company?" she asked me with her pleasant voice.

Of course I didn't say no. The drinks were coming faster, and soon I got a little drunk and a lot horny. She aroused me, and her cleavage was practically forcing me to stare at it. We sat at a table, just the two of us, and when we got more comfortable with each other, her delicate hand touched my leg, going up and under my skirt. With her long nails, she touched my clit. It was enough, just a simple touch, to make my pussy wet. Especially after I fantasized all evening about the two of us eating each other's pussies. She leaned across the table, and I thought that we would kiss right there, but it wasn't a kiss. Instead, she whispered to me that we should go to her place and party on.

That was just what I needed to forget about my useless boyfriend. When we were in the cab, she started to touch my body while she gave me a kinky look and was biting her lips. Slipping her hand under her skirt, she pushed a finger in her vagina, and I realized that she didn't have any panties on. She played with her pussy for a while, still looking at me with pleasure in her eyes. She pulled out of her pussy and the finger that was inside her went straight in her mouth and she sucked on it. That scene from the cab made me so horny that I couldn't wait to arrive at her place and eat out her pussy until I made it squirt all over the place.

The cab suddenly stopped in front of a tall apartment building. Her place was on the last floor, and in the elevator things got really wild. I dropped my purse and we started to kiss aggressively. My hand went straight under her skirt and I began to rub her pussy as hard as I could. When the elevator stopped at the right floor, she was close to an orgasm.

"Don't stop!" She told me. Just after that the elevator's doors opened wide. No one was there, so I decided not to stop. I knelt in front of her and placed my tongue on her fine clit, making the best moves that I knew, just to give her a good orgasm. When she reached her climax, she screamed from the top of her lungs, and soon after that we realized that we were in the hall way of the building and any one could hear us. So we ran as fast as we could in her apartment, sitting behind the closed door and listening to the neighbors who started to exit their homes and check what happened. That was a funny situation for us, and after a good laugh we just stopped and stared in each other's eyes.

"Come with me!" she said, taking my hand and dragging me across the living room and in front of a large window.

The whole wall was a huge window and we started kissing there. Everyone from the adjacent buildings could see us if they wanted. She stripped all the clothes off of me while her lips were kissing my entire body. When just my panties remained, she turned me over and pushed me against the window. My tits were squeezed between my body and the glass, just a perfect view for anyone who wanted something to look at while jerking off. She kissed me slowly from the back of my neck, making my nipples hard. When she was kissing my hips, my panties began to fall off. Using both hands, she spread my butt cheeks and slowly ran her lips over my ass. That was just the beginning, because soon after that, a wild session of pussy and ass eating started. It was a perfect feeling, I was moaning while one of her fingers was penetrating my cunt, and she kept pushing her tongue against my anus, trying to put it in my ass.

She stood up, but she kept fingering me, and her thumb was entering my tight asshole.

"Do you like that, young princess?" She

whispered in my ear while her left hand was slowly choking my neck.

Then she told me to lie down, and from a drawer she took out a big blue rubber dick and a transparent glassy anal dildo. She gave me the blue dick to suck on, and she put the anal dildo in her mouth. She told me to scream if I wanted because the next thing was going to be a little painful. She pushed both of the toys in my holes, one in my pussy and the other in my ass. I felt some pain, but I didn't want to scream. I closed my eyes and waited for the pleasure to come. And that's what happened next. I started to enjoy the hardcore toy fucking. She took out the one from my ass and put it in my mouth while she was licking my enlarged ass hole. She came over to me and covered my face with her pussy, while still fucking me with the fake cock. She gave me the anal dildo to shove it in her ass while she was sitting on my face.

"Faster!" She screamed when the entire dildo was inside her, and with aggressive moves she kept rubbing her pussy in my face.

She didn't need too much to reach an orgasm, and when the second one occurred, with her pussy still on my face, she squirted right in my mouth and all over my face. Mascara tears were dropping from the corner of my eyes, and her pussy juice made my hair soaking wet. Even my tits were covered with it. She got off of me and lay on the floor.

"I want you to squirt all over me," she said with a trembling voice.

I rose, and standing over her I began to rub my clit as hard as I could until all the juice from my pussy came out and flowed onto her gorgeous body. She started to touch herself, and in the next moment her cell phone rang.

"Excuse me, baby, but I got to take this; it's my new boyfriend," she told me.

That was unexpected, but she didn't go in another room to speak. I could hear the voice of the man she was talking to. It sounded very familiar and after she hung up, I asked her what the name of her boyfriend was.

"George," she said, and I almost fainted when I heard that.

"George?! A tall man who's 44 years old? From the suburbs?" I asked her panicked.

"Yes! Why? Do you know him?"

"Do I know him!? He's my fucking father! I can't believe this! I just fucked my father's girlfriend!" I took my clothes from the floor and stormed out the door, naked. I got dressed on the elevator, wondering how something like that happened.

My Friend Lisa

Not knowing what to do, I went in the first bar that I found open. I needed a drink after that, maybe two, which eventually turned to be an entire bottle of vodka. Seeing that I was wasted, the bartender called a cab for me because I could barely speak. So yeah! I was that drunk. When the cab driver asked for the address, the only one that I could give was the one of my good friend Lisa. She was the only one that could understand me and her advice always worked. On top of that, she was the first woman that I ever slept with.

She was a great sex partner with long legs, kind of small but very perky tits, and an ass that made her one of the hottest girls in the entire high school. When we first fucked it was a new thing for both of us. We were two young and horny teenagers, and it happened right after her birthday party when she turned 18. She told me that since it was her birthday that she wanted a special present. I promised I wouldn't refuse anything she asked me, and she asked me for my pussy. It wasn't exactly the normal thing to do, but I did it anyway. We only did that a couple of times because she had a very possessive boyfriend. But since they broke up and my mind was blown away from the fact that I slept with my stepmother, it seemed like a good idea at the time.

Once I got to her place I changed my mind and turned back. My cab was gone and there was no one in the streets. I walked for two minutes when I heard someone calling my name.

"Oh my God, it is you! What are you doing alone in the streets?" Those are the words I heard, and when I looked closer at this strange woman, I realized that it was Lisa.

She saw me at her door and she followed me, not knowing who I was. I tried to explain to her what happened, but being drunk didn't help. So she took me to spend the rest of the night at her place.

The next morning when I woke up, naked in a strange bed, I was a little scared. But then I saw her and I remembered what happened.

"I'm in a really shitty situation, Lisa! I fucked a woman that is supposed to be my stepmom."

"You're still having sex with women? I thought it was just a phase for you, which is why we didn't do it anymore. I'm a lesbian now, I'm done with men. That douchebag ex-boyfriend of mine can go fuck himself because I can't stand to feel another dick in me. Are you lesbian too?" she asked, with hope in her eyes. Telling her that I'm bisexual and didn't want to be in a relationship with a woman was a hard thing to do. She was kind of sad, but she understood me.

"I'm really fucked up right now!" I told her.

"Don't worry, everything is going to be ok! You seem like you need a hug!" She hugged me, but I couldn't resist and my hands slipped down from her back to her perfect ass. When I did this she backed off and looked at me with an expression on her face that could have been translated in: "Are you sure you want to do this?" I leaned forwards, kissed her, and we started to make out. She wasn't so good at it, being the same horny teenager as I remembered. When she put her hand on my clit, I didn't feel a big excitement, and when her finger entered my pussy she scratched me. That was it, I couldn't do that anymore. My mind was drifting to my new stepmom, a real woman, who knew what to do, how to lick a pussy and how to kiss an ass. She knew how to make me cum like Niagara Falls and how to give me pleasure when I'm in pain.

I jumped out the bed and left Lisa's place without any explanation. I can't believe that I left two women like that in a period of 24 hours.

Urge To Fuck

"You know what? Fuck it! Just fuck it!" I kept saying that to myself. The feelings were too strong to resist them. I knew that I only met her last night, but I knew with my entire heart what I must do. Standing in front of her door, I began to have second thoughts. But then the door opened and she was standing in front of me, wearing a beautiful dress that exposed her large cleavage. The dress material was thin and made it very easy to see her pussy and nipples.

"I don't care that you are with my father, I want to be with you too. Can you make that happen?"

"Listen, Ashley, I want to be with you as much as you want, but we need to keep it a secret. Can you do that?"

"Of course I can!" I replied without thinking. A secret relationship with my stepmom sounded weird, but felt right, at least for me. We started to make out with the door open, and she only closed it when all of my clothes were on the floor.

She took me in her bedroom and showed me an entire collection of sex toys from her closet.

"Choose one," she told me.

I went for a black 10-inch dildo. When she saw me with that huge thing in my hand, a smile came across on her face. Then sitting on the bed, her legs widespread, she whispered to me, "Put that thing in my pussy."

I knelt beside the bed and with a sloppy technique I started to lick her pussy and suck on the black rubber cock alternately, wetting it with my saliva so it would slide easily into her perfect MILF cunt. I could tell she was pretty tight down there because it was almost impossible to penetrate her. A scream came from her mouth, followed by her trembling voice telling me to push harder. When the dildo was halfway in her pussy, she ordered me to sit on her face. From what I could tell, she just loved to have a pussy covering her mouth while she screamed of pain and pleasure. And I liked that too, because between screams, her tongue was like a tornado that twisted my clitoris, a feeling of pure bliss.

"I want to feel your hand in me," were the next words that came out of her mouth.

I never tried fisting before, and I wasn't ready to try it now. But since it was not my pussy in the game, I couldn't find a solid argument against it. So I took out the dildo and tossed it to the floor. Her pussy was large enough now to let me slip four fingers in easily.

"What now?" I asked, because the next move was not very clear for me.

My thumb was trying to get in her cunt as well, and I didn't know if I was doing that right. But the confirmation came when she said to me, "Ohh! Don't stop! Don't fucking stop!"

Soon my whole fist was inside her, something that I thought impossible when I first saw her pussy, but there I was. I pushed my hand deeper in her pussy and the waves of her orgasm started, one after another. At the same time her tongue was pleasing my pink asshole, and her finger was rubbing my clit. That finger was the trigger I needed to make me feel the pleasure that I first felt when I was with her. That was the reason that made me wish to be with her that feeling right before the orgasm that only she could offer me.

"I'm such a slut!" I told her right before a river of pussy juice came all over her face.

"We are both sluts, my dear, but we enjoy it!"

She completed me. And she was right. I love to have sex with my stepmom and nothing can stop me from doing it. So far she is the only person that I had slept with and totally enjoyed it. She can make me cum just by fingering my ass and playing with my clit. That's what I call a good catch. Someone that is not afraid to do all kinds of kinky things when in the bedroom. Since that day I continue to fuck my stepmom every time I have the chance.

I love my stepmom

7 BFF ALWAYS SHARE
Monday Night in a Pub

I'm Selena and my life is pretty awesome. In fact, being in college is awesome. My roommate and I are basically living life to its fullest. Carpe diem baby! That's what brought us to the following situation. Jenny, my red-head roommate, loves to party. We hit the clubs three times a week and when we don't feel like clubbing, a pub full of young and drunk people is more than enough for us. It was in a pub like this that a crazy experience began for us.

It was a Monday night. And since everyone hates Mondays, a couple of drinks with Jenny sounded perfect. The pub was much like a sausage fest, only four girls were in there and tons of guys.

ETHEN SHEAR

Jenny, who is a little sex addict, was so happy with the atmosphere. She likes to fuck, a lot. She has at least three or four guys a week, and they all come at our place to bang. Actually, I heard her enough to be able to give scores for the boy's performance based on her moaning. A fine and passionate moaning and I have to admit that more than once it makes me feel very horny and sometimes I like to masturbate listening to the sounds she makes while fucking.

So back to my story, we were drinking at a table when two freshmen boys came over and asked if they could buy us a drink. I thought, "why not?" A long time had passed since I'd been with a freshman. It was in my first year of college. They were super cute, and sometimes they didn't know how to handle the flirt, so we had to take the initiative. Jenny proposed that the first that one who could finish their bottle of beer would get the chance to kiss me. I told her that she was crazy for proposing such a thing, but to be fair I kind of liked the guy who was sitting next to me. His name was Mike and a French kiss from him didn't sound bad, didn't sound bad at all. Fortunately, he was the winner of the challenge and we started kissing right away. Frank, the other guy, who was sitting next to Jenny, asked for a second place prize, and Jenny

82

gave him one, a kiss on the neck that made his young cock get harder. When Jenny saw that, she couldn't hold herself from touching it. With her hand between Frank's legs, he began to change his attitude. One could see on his face that he was horny. I started to like Frank too, but I couldn't decide whom to fuck that night. I was already horny and ready for some action myself.

Mike and Frank's Room

After some more drinks at the pub, the proposal came. They asked us if we wanted to continue the party in their room. I immediately accepted the invitation and Jenny gave it a second thought, but just long enough for Frank to beg her to come.

Their room was not too far from the pub, and we were there in no time. Once we got in, Mike took a bottle of vodka from the fridge. It was ice cold and he asked us if we are in the mood for some body shots. That sounded interesting, so I took off my shirt and jeans to do it. I was wearing a red pair of panties and a red bra. I could say that I was matching with the room because the mood was absolutely crazy. The light was red and that made me feel much more horny than I was at the pub.

He poured some vodka in my belly button, but there was no way for Jenny to let him do those. Once he finished pouring, Jenny took the sip from my belly. She didn't do something like this to me before. I mean I saw her kissing other girls, but her lips never touched my body.

When she looked at me, she winked and I was very surprised. I can't say that I didn't wish for something to happen between us but that was not the way that I expected it to happen. I always imagined that she would get out of the shower with her red hair all wet and I would jump on her in the next moment. Then, we would kiss for a while and eat each other's pussies until we squirted together on each other's faces in a 69 position.

But I couldn't complain about this either. From that moment, I knew that something very kinky was about to happen. And I was right. Soon after that, Frank and Jenny started to make out. They were so intense that my pussy got wet immediately. I was so jealous of my roommate because Mike wasn't that hardcore. In fact, he was a little shy. An awkward silence took over the room and the only sounds that could be heard were the ones produced by Jenny's lips and from time to time her moans because Frank already had his hand in her panties. I waited in vain for Mike to make a move, but I guess he wasn't that experienced with girls. The only thing that I could do was to sit there and wait. It never occurred to me that I could give him stronger signals to let him understand that I wanted his tongue on my clit. My luck was Jenny's attention. She managed, somehow, to take a glance at the two of us and when she saw that nothing was happening between us, she decided to give us a little help.

"Let's play another game! If Selena and I will go topless, you guys will have to go bottomless."

"What?!" I replied, shocked as if I didn't even wanted something to happen.

"Trust me Selena! It's the only way," she replied with a whisper.

So we went topless and Frank took off his pants. He wasn't wearing any underwear, and his cock was hard enough to hang laundry on it. He was uncut, something that I don't really like in boys. But Mike was hesitating and I was a little disappointed. I really liked this guy, but he was too shy. It was time to do something about it, so I poured him a couple shots of tequila and I placed them between my tits which were squashed by my hands, and I walked slowly and provocatively towards him.

"Drink it!" I commanded him like a kinky dominatrix.

After vanishing those shots, he took the bottle of tequila from the table and drank half of it in just one sip. Once finished, he poured some of it on my tits and began to lick it off. That was something new. It was like I was facing another person. In the next moment, his pants were flying across the room and when I looked down to his crotch I was amazed. A long and beautiful dick was revealed from under his shirt, and when I say long, I mean it. It was so thick and big that I could easily choke by only sucking half of it.

The Party Begins

We were standing face to face, speechless, and desiring wild sex in our eyes. From the couch, Frank and Jenny were watching us like they didn't know what would happen next. So in that moment, I knew it was my chance to be wilder then my red-head best friend with the slutty attitude. So without any warning, I kneeled in front of Mike and like in porn movies, I began to suck his big fat dick. I have to admit, that my hunger for cock made me suck on it like a professional hooker. Frank was blocked on the view and I bet he wanted to be in Mike's place and look down at the super kinky face that I make when I have a real sausage in my mouth.

Jenny was obviously jealous of me because I eclipsed her with my excellent blow job skills. So she proposed another game. Her idea was to place the boys on the couch, one beside another so we can make a dick-sucking contest. I was ok with that because I didn't want her to think that I was a bitch who tried to steal the moment. So with the boys sitting on the couch, we proceed to the sucking cock competition. Jenny was very competitive, and while she was "performing" her eyes were filled with hate. Not a real hate, but a kind of pounding my ass with a dildo as a punishment hate. That side of Jenny was so awesome that I wanted to see more, so I pretended to care about the blow job contest, just to see her reactions.

Things heated up between us and soon enough she wasn't playing anymore and she stopped from sucking Frank's cock just to yell at me.

"Do you think that you could have better oral skills than me? I'll show you what oral really means!" And she pushed me on the floor and in the next second, her beautiful red head was between my legs. With her tongue all over my pussy, I didn't care anymore that there were someone else in the room. Moaning like a Japanese teen from porn movies, I placed my hand in her hair, just to keep her mouth on my pussy until I could orgasm. It didn't take long and I have to admit that her oral skills were brilliant. I squirted all over her face and the mascara start to drip in tears on her cheeks.

She rose over me and said, "Who's the champion now? Bitch!"

"You are, my love" I said to her, glad that it finally happened and with the hope in my heart that it wasn't the only time when I get to be licked by my best friend.

"Now I need some cock! Frank, don't you dare cum!" She ordered.

Now Jenny was on top of Frank, riding on his junk like a cowgirl. I was still laid on the floor, with a hand on my pussy, when I realized that I could get more pleasure right away. Looking at Mike, I told him to come closer. Fortunately, he understood what I meant and came right away. With him on top of me, I could feel his hard cock touching my pussy, so I took it in my hand and started to rub my clit with the tip of the dick. It was terrific, and if you read this, you should definitely try it someday. It felt so good that I couldn't restrain myself and let my entire pussy juice stream all over his dick and balls.

Once I finished squirting, I dragged him over me, put my hands around him and whispered in his ear, "Fuck me as hard as you can!"

That was all he wanted to hear, I guess, because it was like he released some kind of sex demon from deep inside his soul. He was pounding my tight pussy with that huge cock of his, and the moaning that we both produced made Jenny and Frank stop from what they were doing and join us in a group fuck.

Jenny put her pussy on my face and started to move her hips, which made my task easier and sexier. Meanwhile, Frank went in front of her and asked if she could handle a throat fuck. She was ok with it; I knew it because the sound of her gagging on a dick could be heard many times in our home. Once Frank pushed his cock down Jenny's throat, the orgy was complete. Her saliva mixed with mascara tears dripped all over my hair, something that normally would gross me out. But in that moment, it was a perfect feature of our love square.

After a while, we decided to switch partners, so Mike took Jenny and put her doggy style on the couch and I laid back on the rest of the couch, with my head right over Jenny's face. When the guys started to fuck us, we made eye contact and the moaning turned into screams of pleasure. In the heat of the moment, I asked my best friend to spit in my mouth, and after she did, we begun kissing while our pussies were fucked by two strong freshmen boys. I didn't ever want that scene to end. Playing with her bouncing tits reminded me that the night was started as a typical Monday, but it turned out to something so awesome that I wanted it to be a regular thing. So between screams and orgasms, I found the power to ask if we could do this every week on Mondays. Of course, the boys were ok with that, but Jenny looked at me and said:

"Looks like someone enjoys being fucked like a whore! I like that about you, Selena."

That was it; Jenny and I were a fuck team from that moment. I couldn't wait to arrive home and have our little adventures together. The thought of having a bisexual roommate that I could fuck from now on made me have another orgasm. When I began to squirt, Frank, who sensed it, went down on me and took all my pussy juice in his mouth then spit it all over my body. When Jenny saw that, she immediately licked some of it off my tits and sucked my nipples while Frank was licking my clit with his tongue. Mike, who was behind Jenny, stopped fucking her pussy and began licking her ass. When I saw that, it made me want that too. I told Frank that I wanted to be fucked in the mouth too, but he could only do it with one condition: Jenny and I would swap their sperm when they cum. It seemed like a fair deal, but I didn't know if I accepted because I wanted to make some cum swapping with the girl who was licking my butt or because I couldn't wait to be mouth fucked.

After that, they told us to kneel on the floor and their dicks were soon sucked dry. I have to admit that Jenny is a better cock sucker than me because she made Frank cum first. Because she did that, she won the chance to take Mike's cum too. I was jerking off Mike while the tip of his dick was in Jenny's mouth. Once he came, my red-head kinky friend had two big loads of sperm in her mouth; sperm which she let drip on my lips and face. After her mouth was empty, she started to lick it off my face and we kissed with our lips covered in sperm. I managed to swallow a little because a large amount of semen dripped on our tits.

Mike asked us to sit there and smile for a photo. After he took the photo, I could see how much me and Jenny looked like two dirty sluts. I liked that!

From that night on, our gang of four meets every Monday night for an old-fashion orgy, and sometimes we use toys and lots of costumes. I like when Jenny played the role of a dominatrix and punished me by making the guys fuck me, one in the pussy and another one in the ass. That's right! I enjoy anal now. And this is the story of how I began to explore my sexual life at its finest.

8 SEX, DRUGS & ROCK 'N ROLL

The Drive

It was a summer day when I received an e-mail from an online rock community that I'm a member of. The e-mail said that a concert was scheduled for that night not far from my town, and since I had nothing to do, I decided to go for it. But when I looked in my wallet, I only had money for the ticket and a pack of cigarettes. I'm a 19-year-old blonde girl, with big boobs and a naughty ass, and there's no way I can't manage to get a free ride to the concert. My name is Joanne by the way, and I'm a big rock fan, and this is the story of how I started a sexual adventure.

Before leaving the house, I had to make

sure that I was attractive enough to be picked up off the road by someone with a car. A black sleeveless leather jacket with just a bra underneath, a short skirt and high-heeled boots was enough for me to stop any car that I wanted to. Ready for the party, I left the house and walked down the street until I left my small town. Once I got on the open road, I spotted a van with a sexy punk girl driving. I waved at her, and she immediately stopped the van and waited for me to approach. In the back of the van were two guys and another girl, all punk rockers.

"Going to the Bone Head concert?" asked the girl that was driving the van.

"Yes, my name is Joanne! What's your name?" I asked her back.

"I'm Tasha, the other girl is Anya and the boys are Rob and Toby."

"Are you couples or something?" Curiosity pushed me to ask.

"Or something." Tasha said.

That gave me something to think about, because I didn't quite understand what she meant to say. We had a three-hour drive ahead, and I didn't want to spend the entire time asking questions about them. Fortunately, Toby took out a bag of weed from the glove box and asked if I smoked. I'm a big pot head, but just for fun, I told him that I don't smoke weed. He began to explain that his weed was a good strain, and I was curious about what strain I was about to smoke. When he said that the weed was Moby Dick, I couldn't keep my mouth shut and said:

"Hmmmm... I love dick!"

"You only love dick?" Anya asked right away.

I'm a bisexual so I know one when I see one, and the two punk girls were as bisexual as you get. Since I decided to go wild on this trip, I told Anya that I would answer her if she closed her eyes. When she did, I gave her a kiss on the lips, and once she was sure that I was into that, her hand went right under my skirt. The boys were not as surprised as I thought they would be, but that's because they were familiar with this kind of scene, I guess.

When the joints were ready, everybody lit one up and I did the same. After a couple of minutes, everything changed. The van had such a sexual tension that I couldn't take it anymore. I wanted something to happen, but there was no way for me to initiate it. So I just gave them a hint, I told them that it was too hot for me and I took off my jacket. My big boobs looked perfect that day, and I could see how Rob was undressing me with his eyes. Anya saw it too, and I guess there was something between them, because she got a little jealous, so she took off her shirt too. She had the better breasts because she was wearing no bra and her tits looked gorgeous. Not as big as mine, but she had a tribal tattoo on her left boob and both nipples were pierced.

"You're full of piercings! Do you have any more?" I asked her convinced that her clit was pierced too.

She didn't answer me, but she took my hand and placed it under her skirt to feel the round metal ring that was attached to her pussy. Her gesture made me wet my bikini and I wasn't shy to admit it. After we finished the joints, I put my hand through her pink hair and we made out in the back of the van until it stopped moving.

"Why are we stopping?" I asked Tasha.

"Because I want to be a part of it too." She replied with a kinky tone that left me with the impression that something big was about to happen.

The van was big enough to fit the three of us girls and had space for the two guys if they wanted to join us. I started making out with Tasha while Anya was taking off my bra and my skirt, and she even rubbed my pussy through my bikini. I hadn't been this wet in a long time, so I took off my bikini, and after that I didn't care what was about to happen as long as pussy juice was coming out of me.

All of a sudden Anya, who was beside me, grabbed Tasha by her black hair and shoved her face into my pussy. It was quite aggressive and scared me a little. If she wasn't making my tight pussy so wet I might have stopped her, but I told myself that there is no way I could stop now. Not when I was enjoying this exciting lesbian threesome that was amplified by the high that the weed gave me.

Between my moans, I could hear Anya tell the boys to come closer. Toby was in front of me and Rob in front of Anya. At her command, they took out their penises. Toby had a nice cock, not too big, but not too small either. It was just fine for me to suck on it. Anya began to blow and jerk off Rob while with the other hand she continued to hold Tasha's head between my legs. I looked at Anya and I tried to tell her that I wanted to lick some pussy too, but there was no way for me to say anything, cause I was no longer just sucking Toby's dick, I was getting mouth fucked. When I almost had an orgasm, the tongue that was doing such a good job on my pussy disappeared. Anya took Tasha away from me and shoved her down on herself to eat out her pierced pussy.

"Looks like you want to lick some pussy too." Anya told me, and I nodded my head trying to say yes because Toby's dick was down my throat.

"You can lick off Tasha's pussy and ass if you want to," she replied.

So I went behind Tasha who was bent over doggy style, with her head between Anya's legs. I lifted up her skirt and I noticed that she wasn't wearing undies either. Her pussy looked perfect from behind, and soon enough, I was pushing my tongue inside her butt hole. At the same time, my middle finger was stuffing her cunt and my thumb was rubbing her pussy. I could hear her moaning, and when I looked at Anya, she was performing such a fantastic blowjob on both of the guys. Tasha tried to tell me something, and I could only guess that she was talking about me putting my fingers in her ass. I put the tip of my finger in her, but she took my hand and pushed it deeper into her ass. I knew then that she wanted to feel some pain as well. If it was pain she wanted, pain is what she'd get. I began by aggressively pushing two fingers inside her, and I wanted to get my whole fist in, but she stopped me at four fingers and told Toby to fuck her in the ass. Meanwhile, Rob ravished Anya's pussy on the wall of the van.

I was alone, with no one to fuck, so the only option was to fuck myself. My fingers were enough to make me squirt all over the floor of the van. I was a little surprised when I saw how Tasha, who was not so far from me, started to lick the pussy juice that was slowly draining away under her face.

They continued to fuck and I kept pleasuring myself, but there had to be a way to get some cock inside of me. It made me very frustrated and the only reason for me to stick with them was the free ride to the concert and probably the fact that I was extremely horny and still hoped to be fucked. For ten minutes, they ignored me, until Anya told me to come closer. I thought that it was my turn to be ridden. Unfortunately, that wasn't it; instead, she called me there so that the boys could cum on all our faces. It was a very disappointing orgy that it made me wish we would arrive soon to the concert to find someone who could fuck me well. We swapped the sperm a couple of times, and then Tasha took her place at the wheel of the car and drove away, all naked and covered in cum.

The Concert After Party

Once the car stopped where the concert was held, I got out and left without saying anything. After paying for my ticket, I went straight to the beer stand and waited for some handsome rocker to buy me a drink. Dressed the way I was, I didn't have to wait too long for a tall guy with dark long hair, wearing nothing but army boots and jeans, came over to me. He asked me if I was interested in having a drink with him, but he also asked for something else in return for the free beer. He was talking about a kiss, but I was too horny for kisses so I told him that I could offer more than just a kiss. We enjoyed our beers, and after much small talk that was laced with sexual tension, he told me that the band that was playing that night was having a private party at the hotel and he could take me there as his plus one.

Things were getting pretty good; we drank some more beers, smoked some pot and enjoyed the concert. I had such a great time with this guy, whose name I still didn't know, but it was better that way because the mystery increased the excitement. When the concert was over, he took me to his car and drove me to the hotel where the party was.

We arrived a little late because we stopped by the road to smoke another joint before the party and got carried away by some music. When we got there, the party had already started. There was enough booze and coke for everyone, so I took a couple of tequila shots and sniffed some of the finest coke I'd ever had. It made me go crazy and filled me with energy. I danced around all night, and when I decided to change the rhythm, I took the guy who invited me and went to find a room, because I was desperate to fuck something. Almost all the rooms were closed, and when we finally found one that was open, there was no light inside. I search for a switch to turn on the light, and when I found it, I saw an older couple fucking like dogs. He was around 40 and she was 35, drunk and high on coke. I asked them if we could join. They looked at me and the woman was thrilled at the thought that she could be in a foursome. I went straight to her and we started kissing. Meanwhile, my guy, who I'll call Chuck, started undressing me. The first thing he did when he finished was stick his cock deep inside my pussy. I didn't see his dick, but from the way it felt inside my pussy, I could tell that he was pretty hung.

The strange woman was lying on the bed with her partner's cock in her ass while I was bent over, doggy style, beside her, getting seriously fucked by Chuck. She asked Chuck if he and her partner could double penetrate her in the ass, and in no time, two strong phalluses were stuffing her pretty large butt hole. I was dick-less again, so the only thing to do was to sit with my pussy on the punk MILF's face. She had perfect oral skills, and the view from on top of her was gorgeous. Breasts like two volley balls and a pierced clit made me orgasm really fast.

I'm a squirter, and it wasn't too hard for me to let my juices gush directly into her mouth. I could hear her swallowing it, and I think she liked the taste because she said that a little more of my orgasmic liquid would make her happy. I bent over just to get my tongue onto that perfect pussy of hers. It was visible all over her body that she liked fucking a lot, but that didn't mean that she was a cheap slut. I think she was just a little nympho, because she kept screaming that she wanted to be fucked harder. While licking her pussy, I inserted three of my fingers inside of her. Only that made her orgasm, but even then, she was screaming for more.

I was asked by the older guy if I wanted to try anal with him. I'm always up for it, since I like a little pain too. But my condition was that Chuck had to fuck my tight pussy at the same time; only then would I let him fuck me in the ass. Of course, they were up to it. Besides, I was a fine young girl with no inhibitions and an awesomely hot body. Chuck laid on his back and I went cowgirl on him. The other mysterious man slowly pushed his fat cock up my ass as little tears of pain started to drip from the corner of my eyes, but I didn't want to stop. Like I said, a little pain is enjoyable. So when I was ready to have my ass destroyed, I yelled at the top of my lungs:

"Push it harder motherfucker!!!"

He did exactly what I said. At that moment, I started screaming like a little girl, and I'm not sure if the screams were caused by pain or pleasure, or a combination of the two. I wasn't able to say anything kinky anymore, so I told them to have their way with me, but to make sure that I orgasmed. The other woman liked the idea and wanted to be used like a sex toy as well, so we sat on the bed and let them face fuck us until they came all over our faces.

When they finally released their sperm onto our beautiful faces and bodies, we started to lick it off each other. After that, I took my clothes and burst out the door. Tired, wasted and fucked like a slut, I started to walk home and wait for someone to pick me up off the side of the road. It was a crazy day in which I was involved in two orgies, but I don't regret any of them. I hope that I'll find more concerts like this one, because a good old fashion pussy destroying session doesn't compare to any pleasure that a single man could offer. Not even if his dick was made of pure gold and his cum was liquid happiness. I can't wait to be an unknown slut again, but next time, I want to get fucked by a whole rock band. I think I'll become a groupie; it isn't a glamorous life but at least the sex is fucking awesome.

9 IMMORTAL LOVE
The Curse

It was a summer night in the countryside of Transylvania, when a loud voice could be heard right outside my little house. It was the voice of Ekaterina, the wife of the man who fucked me in the last two months. She found out about our secret, and her anger was coming upon me in form of an ancient spell.

Everybody thought she was a witch, but I refused to believe that. Maybe because her husband was such a stallion, I was afraid for this to happen, but I could not stop from having amazing sex with him at the time. She kept saying something in a strange language, and since nothing was happening, I choose to ignore her. My peace didn't last long, and in the first night, with a full moon, the curse came upon me and it was awful. The year was 1655 when my fangs appeared and the hunger for blood took over all my body. The fucking bitch turned me into a vampire, and there was nothing I could do except for hunting. So I started to chase people. The thought of killing innocent people drove me crazy, so I choose to suck the blood of the old and the weak ones who would die in a few days anyway. It didn't work, it only helped to calm me down for a couple of hours. But when the hunger occurred again, it was even bigger. There was a second urge that appeared after a while. I was horny almost all the time, but not normal horny, I wanted to fuck at any price.

After a month of walking around at night, scared and concerned, I finally managed to lure a young man in the woods, because I wasn't able to restrain myself from fucking anymore. When he took down his pants, I jumped on him right away. He was so young and beautiful, his cock was fine for his age, and we started to fuck like two dogs in heat. Somehow, by mistake I think, he stuck his dick in my ass, and that was the moment when I realized that I wasn't able to feel pain anymore. I wanted to stop, but my body wasn't listening to me anymore. I continued to ride his strong manhood that was going deep inside my tight ass, and I couldn't feel a thing except pure joy. It was the first time that I felt alive since the curse was set over me. When he put this cock back in my pussy, I could feel how the orgasm took over my body. I started trembling and screaming like a wolf. The young boy was so scared that he wasn't able to cum and his erection was gone. After the orgasm stopped, I looked him in the eyes and without realizing it I just bit his neck and let all his blood burst in my mouth. It was pure magic in that moment, and I only realized what I did after the poor boy was dead. I felt terrible for what I just did, but at the same time, I felt great, because my hunger and my urge to fuck were gone.

It lasted nine days time, in which I discovered that I had some sort of power. I could hear better and my smell was intensified. I was able to smell the erection of a man from huge distances, and after the nine days had passed, the urges appeared again. I discovered that the only thing that could stop my hunger was the blood of a good-looking man that I was fucking. So I did the same thing over and over for more than 60 years. After all the years, I didn't age a day. My dark hair and eyes, my big round boobs, my perfect ass and my tight pink pussy made many men fall into the trap of deadly sex. I was still as young and beautiful as I was when the witch cursed me for being a slut, at the age of 23. I think that this is the reason why I could only feed on the blood of handsome men that I fuck.

Everything was good as it was. I accepted the thought that I would never be normal again. I was living on the roads, sleeping in the inns all over the country and moving around after every feeding. I made my money stealing from my victims and I got used to that kind of life.

Someone Like Me

After hundreds of men died with their dicks stuck in my pussy, I was sure of what I was doing, so planning wasn't something I had to do. I just stood beside a road that was far enough from the village and waited for a man to pass by. While sitting there, a silhouette was coming toward me. A tall man with long blond hair and big arms was going to be my next victim. When he got closer to me, I asked him if I could offer him some pleasure in exchange of his money. I knew he would accept, and we started kissing in the dark road. I took his hand and dragged him slowly in the woods where he pushed me on the ground and lifted my dress to put his mouth on my cunt. No one did that to me before, because in that time, it was considered a sin to perform oral sex, except one man. When he finished licking my pink pussy, he raised his head from between my legs and the moon made possible for me to see a face that shocked me so bad that I wanted to run right away. But I realized that we were in a dark wood and only I could see his face, he couldn't, so I kept my mouth shut. Afraid, I stood there while he put his big strong cock inside my pussy. The pleasure that he was able to give me using his manhood was so intense that I couldn't resist anymore and by mistake I whispered his name, James. That was the moment of truth. James was the husband of Ekaterina, the witch that cursed me to become a vampire forever. He immediately stopped fucking me and said, "Mish!? How can you...you are a vampire too?"

"Yes my darling, I'm Mish. And I can see that your bitch wife also turned you into a vampire. But I'm glad we can still be back together. I hope that you want that too." I said to him, with tears in my eyes.

In that moment, he didn't say anything. The only thing that he could do was to keep fucking me. It was a wild thing to do, judging by the fact that we were both vampires and our instinct was to eat each other. Under the sky that was turning brighter and brighter, he put me on my feet facing a tree and started to fuck me from behind. We were both moaning, but our moans were in fact scary screams that could be heard from miles away. I had lots of orgasms that made me really happy for the first time in 60 years. When almost finished, I kneeled in front of him and put his cock in my mouth, sucking on it and waiting for his sweet sperm to burst right down my throat. I swallowed his cum, and when all was over, we barely restrained ourselves from eating each other.

Years had passed since then, and we were still young and more powerful. There was no way of having sex just the two of us, because our wild instincts would make us attack each other, and in the best case scenario, we would have died together. So we developed a technique that allowed us to fuck and eat at the same time. We lured young couples like us in our house to make them be part of an orgy, and that's how we met a couple that knew much more than we could imagine.

A Strange Couple

We met Tony and Jena in the winter of 2010, in a Goth club where we used to hang out at night. They were so in love but so sexual at the same time. We started talking with them, and Jena kissed me out of the blue. I knew what that meant, so I invited them to our home, a big house in a suburb near LA. We arrived there, and Tony started to kiss me, and Jena went straight for James's cock. I stood there and watched how a mortal woman was blowing the love of my life, while I got stuck with an idiot we just met. I got so angry that I could have eaten them right away. But I knew that wasn't a smart move, so just to tease my love, I started to suck Tony's penis. We got carried away pretty fast, and before I knew it, the guys were standing beside me with their cocks in my hands and Jena was licking my pussy like a real lesbian. I got too horny to be jealous anymore so I asked the guys to fuck us. This time, Tony was fucking Jena, and James was all mine. I was on top of him and Tony was pounding Jena right behind me, doggy style, a position that allowed her to lick my tight, pink ass hole. Since she was enjoying so much my ass, I had a kinky idea. I asked the guys if they could double penetrate my butt and they did that. Now Jena was just sitting there, fingering herself and watching me getting fucked intensely. They noticed that our moans were, in fact, wild screams, but they thought it was just a sex game. I demanded both of the guys cum in my ass, because I wanted to humiliate Jena before I eat her. In no time, my butt hole was full of sperm, and I turned my back to Jena, put my ass near her mouth, grabbed her long red hair and pushed her face between my butt cheeks. I was really proud that I made her swallow all the cum that was coming right from the inside of my ass. And after she swallowed everything, just to humiliate her more, I slapped her twice and called her a "good bitch".

James and I were set to start feeding ourselves with their blood, and when we revealed our big and scary fangs, they started to run around our house and scream. Between tears, Jena told us that she knows what could break the curse that was set upon us. That phrase made me stop from hunting her down and listened to her.

"I know what kind of curse was brought upon you two. I can help you fix it if you want. Just please let me and Tony live!" said Jena, crying her soul out.

I was curious for what she was about to say, because I wished so bad to be mortal again, to live my life in a normal way and most importantly to be able to make love to James. She said that she has some old magic books from Transylvania and she found a potion that could break any vampiric curse. She knew the ingredients for the potion and she told us. We needed blood from a lamb, hair from a virgin, apple seeds and tears from the whispering eye of the witch that cursed us. She knew how to get all the ingredients, except for the tears. She didn't know what whispering eye means. But luckily, I was born in 1632 and I knew that whispering eye was another name for cunt. But the hard part was to get the pussy juice of the witch that turned us this way.

"There is no hope. Who knows when that Ekaterina bitch died?" James said, with a lot of anger in his voice.

"Did you say Ekaterina? Isn't that the vendor that sold you the magic books, Jena?" asked Tony.

"Yes! Yes it is! And I can show you where she lives, and besides, she is a lesbian. How do you think I paid for the books? A witch can make the spell only twice, and she will live as long as the curse is not broken."

So Jena showed me where Ekaterina lived, and I went straight there with a fake reason. Fortunately, she didn't recognize me and I fabricated a story in which I was a lesbian and my girlfriend left me for a man. So I wanted to put a curse on her and so on. After she told me a spell for it I started to cry and jumped in her arms. Being such a hot young girl, she couldn't resist kissing me and that was my shot. I pretended to be shy at first, but just enough to keep her hitting on me. She pleased her hand between my legs and started to rub my clit while I stood there with the thought that I could kill her right there, in that very moment. But I didn't do it, because I wanted to be normal much more, and when all would be done she would die anyway.

When she was horny enough, I started to make my move. I began with a simple kiss on the lips and continued by taking off all her clothes and tossed her on the floor. I spread her legs wide open while my lips were getting closer and closer to her pussy. When I had her clit in my mouth, I began to suck and lick it. I tried to do my best and I did. In no time, she had a massive orgasm that made her squirt like a waterfall. In that moment when her eyes were closed, because she was enjoying what I was doing, I took out a little bottle from my purse, which was near me and collect a few drops of her pussy juice. That was enough for me to make the potion, but I couldn't leave. Not without making her suspicious. So I took down my skirt and panties and I got on top of her, putting my pussy on her face and making the simple act of breathing a little difficult for her. I was rubbing my clit while she was trying to get her tongue inside my pussy, just to make sure that I could have an orgasm. After I squirted all over her bitchy face, I pretended that I got scared and left her house like a shy girl.

When I arrived home, we began to make the potion. I was so nervous when we both drank it that I almost fainted. In a short time, the hunger passed and our senses came back to normal. We were mortals again. Finally, after all these years, we could be a couple who could make love and live happy. Since that moment, we decided to live our life to its fullest and we started traveling around the globe, meeting nice people and having sex on the various beaches, like any other young couple. The only exception was that we had been in love since 1655, and we could finally enjoy our love in peace.

10 PASSION RUNS IN

Virginity: Gone

My name is Monica and I love my adopted brother's best friend, Jason. I'm a 22-year-old hot girl, with medium-sized breasts and a huge appetite for sex. I can't say that I'm a slut, but I keep a huge secret. When Jason was still 19 years old—that's two years ago—I discovered that he is a real stallion. Let me tell you the story of about us.

We live with our adopted mother in a house in the suburbs ever since our adopted dad left us for a hooker, and my adopted brother Peter was the man in the house. We grew up together like brother and sister, but he would bring home his best friend who was getting hotter and hotter and I guess he was thinking the same about me. Attracted to him big time, I used to watch through the door whenever Jason would slepover with Peter. I would often catch Jasonas he would masturbate. But it was the one time I was playing with my pussy, in the comfort of my bed, that our little secret started. I had a yellow vibrator that made my lonely days full of orgasms, and it was jammed in my cunt when I noticed that the door from my room, which was cracked open, moved a little.

"Jason, is that you? Don't be shy. Come in!" I told him with a really sexy voice.

And he entered the room. He was naked from bottom down because he was jerking off while watching me play with my toy. He was blushing like a lobster and I told him to come closer and sit on the bed.

"Hey Jason, do you watch me often?" I asked him like it was no big deal.

"Only when I hear you moan, Monica. But please! Don't tell your brother! Please!" He responded with a scared and shy voice.

"It's OK, little Jason. I won't tell if you won't tell. You know, I used to watch you from outside the window when you watched porn and Peter. I have to tell you, you have a nice, big cock. The girls you fuck with that cock are probably so happy."

"I'm still a virgin, Monica."

"Oh! My poor Jason! That's not good at all! We have got to fix this right away."

And that was the moment when I leaned down to his crotch and took his entire dick in my mouth. It was really big and straight because the top of it jammed down my throat, making me gag a little bit. I could hear in his moans that he was a little bit of afraid, but he loved what was happening because he leaned back on the bed, letting me blow him freely. Without saying a word, I got on top of him, and with my hand, I placed Jason's dick inside my pussy. Looking him in the eyes, I let myself go down slowly on his dick until all of it was in my little cunt. Then I started fucking him. It was so good that the first orgasm occurred only after three or four minutes. I never had such wonderful sex before, and I think that it was because Jason was my brother's best friend.

The passion and the adrenaline were at maximum levels. I took his hands and placed them on my tits because I like to be touched while I'm on top. After a while, he got a little courage, tossed me on the bed, and came over me. His dick was slowly penetrating me and he leaned over my face until our lips touched together in an intense kiss. We started to make out and fuck very wildly, and the lucky part was that we were home alone—the screams of pleasure that we were both making could be heard in the entire house. I knew that it wasn't normal to be fucked by my brother's best friend, but the fact that he was fucking me so good has to count for something. The only regret I had in those passionate moments was that I didn't let Jason fuck me before. He was a real talent. I like sex and I had a lot of it, with a lot of men and even women, but I never felt such powerful orgasms. He suddenly stopped and remained frozen; I thought that he came inside of me but I didn't feel anything like that. The problem was that he wanted to lick my pussy, but he didn't know how to ask. I simply put my hand on his head and pushed him down between my legs. When he was there, he became a real tornado with his long and sharp tongue. That tornado became a hurricane very soon; being horny and all, I started to squirt out a lot of pussy juice right on his face and in his mouth. Being kinky and all, I asked him to swallow my juice and kiss me.

I guessed he could not fuck me anymore so I put him on the side of the bed and I kneeled in front of him between his legs. While I was jerking him off, the tip of his cock was right on my lips, so when he orgasmed, all his sweet sperm burst into my mouth. And it was a huge load of cum. I gave him a little show, playing with his sperm and licking all that had been left on his dick and on my lips. At the end, I swallowed it in a very hot manner and I thanked him for the sweet treat.

We started kissing when I heard the front door open. It was my adopted mother that came back from shopping. I gave him his shirt and sent him to my brother's room very fast. My bed was all wet from squirting, so I covered the spot with a pillow, dressed real fast, and went downstairs.

Peter's Birthday

From time to time, Jason and I would fuck. We even went for a weekend to the beach side together and Peter never knew. I knew that it's insane to be a fuck buddy of my adopted brother, best friend but it was so good that I couldn't help myself. One morning when it was Peter's birthday, and Jason had slept over, I decided to surprise him with a good morning sex session after Peter left for a while. I thought we were alone so I went to Peter's room to find Jason, and while he was sleeping, I got under the blanket and started to suck on his magnificent cock. He woke up moaning and pulled the blanket down off me just to drag me on top of him. We began to fuck so hard that the bed was hitting the wall and making loud sounds that were covered only by my screams of pleasure. Jason asked me to let him fuck my tight ass. How could I say no him and his magnificent cock? So I got my ass prepared for his big cock and positioned for doggy style. I waited for him to penetrate my ass, but he was a gentleman. Before even putting his dick near my ass, he placed his face between my butt cheeks and started to lick my hole. It was a wonderful feeling; I mean, I've been licked there before by a girl from college, but this time it was my brother's best friend Jason and everything was perfect. First he pushed a finger in my ass, gentle and careful. There was a little pain, but the pleasure was high.

Right before he could get his cock inside of me, a loud noise came from behind us. It was our mother's best friend, Lacy who would come check on the house who busted us. I thought she would be crazy mad, but her reaction was not the one that I was expecting. She stood there and said:

"Don't stop just because I'm here! I've always noticed how you two had the hots for each other. You better not let your brother Peter find out. Anyway, I was certain that this would eventually happen. I know I shouldn't ask something like this, but can I join you?"

My mind was blown away. How could

Lacy be okay with this? I don't know why she wouldn't want to tell my brother or mom. I don't even know how she could be that calm over this. How could she ask us if she could join? She told me that she could teach me some nice tricks for blowjobs. I couldn't say no—that's how shocked I was. The situation got out of control and I felt like dying of shame. But she approached me and placed her hand on my naked body. The way that she touched me was great. I could tell by the look on her face that she knew what she was doing and she was quite experienced. When her hand touched my pussy, I had a very weird feeling. It was some sort of pleasure mixed with fear, anger, and shame. It made my pussy wet like the first time Jason touched me with his tongue down there.

"Now let's teach you how to properly suck a dick!" Lacy said. With one hand, she was rubbing my clitoris, and with the other one, she was jerking off Jason.

I thought that it would be some sort of a nightmare if she told Peter or my mom, but now it was okay. I decided that I had to let go of all my emotions and enjoy a threesome. She grabbed me by the hair and pushed me towards my Jason's cock. She told me to open my mouth wide, and when I did, her hand pushed my head so that his dick went straight to my throat. I restrained myself from gagging. Seeing this, Lacy congratulated me. We both sucked Jaon's big cock for some time, and I even French kissed her. It was strange, but the excitement in the room was intense.

Until now I never had any sexual interactions with a MILF, and when I had my first, it was with my adopted mother's best friend. I can't say that I didn't like it. In fact, Lacy was a very hot MILF. She had blue eyes and long blond hair. Her huge tits look perfect; her tanned skin and ass are absolutely gorgeous. I never had the chance to see her pussy. But just when I was thinking of that, she told me that she wanted to suck my Jason's dick while I performed oral on her. How could I say no to her? So I lifted her skirt up to see that she wasn't wearing any underwear. Her pussy looked exactly like mine; the years were kind to her. She was a 44-year-old with a pussy of a 22-year-old girl. I was glad that Lacy had such a pussy, and after I began to lick it, I'm sure she was glad that I had such a talented mouth. I say this because I could hear her moaning with Jason's cock down her throat. He was moaning too, and when I looked up, I could see that he wasn't scared anymore either because his hands were on Lacy's head and he was practically face fucking her. Drool was dripping from her mouth right on to her big boobs, and from time to time, she played with her saliva-covered tits.

I tried to give my Lacy an orgasm. My next move was to put two fingers inside of her. After I fingered her pretty hard, she finally came. My mouth was on her pussy when that happened, so I had a huge load of pussy juice gush into my mouth. I chose to spit all the pussy juice over my mother's face just to be completely nasty.

She asked Jason to fuck her like how he fucked me before. Lacy was on her back and Jason was fucking her like a porn star. I covered her face with my round ass, still wanting to be pounded by my Jason. Lacy had some experience in this matter too because she knew what to do with her tongue and her finger in order to make my asshole happy.

The pleasure was so intense but it wasn't enough. So I placed my fingers in my pussy and started to masturbate while my Lacy was giving me anal pleasure. Soon after that, I had an orgasm and my pussy squirted bursts of juice on my mother's blond hair. Now her hair was soaking wet; that made her look even more hot and kinky. After she had a couple of orgasms, it was my turn to be satisfied by Jason. She told me to lie on my back and she took his dick in her hand and placed it right at the entrance of my ass. Then she got on top of me and we were in a 69 position while Jason was fucking me in the ass. The anal and oral sex was so great that I had continuous orgasms for more than ten minutes. The bed beneath us was all wet, and I think that the moans and screams could have been heard by all the other neighbors. But we didn't care. It was too much pleasure to care about such a thing at the time.

From time to time, Lacy would pull Jason's cock out of my ass and suck on it, and then she would put it back in my ass, telling him to push deeper and harder. That made me scream more, but it didn't hurt at all. Lacy told Jason that if he wanted to finish, he could finish inside of me. And after a few minutes, I could hear him making the sounds that he makes when he is about to orgasm and I could feel his hot sperm inside me.

She asked me to squat and to push the cum out of my ass while her face was right between my legs. All the sperm burst out of my ass and directly on her face. She came in front of me and I understood that I had to lick all the sperm off her beautiful skin. I did that, but she told me to keep it in my mouth and to not swallow it. Then she kissed Jason on his cock. After that she came beside me and looked at my Jason, telling him that the next scene was for him. We started kissing with all the cum from my mouth covering our lips. We swapped the sperm a couple of times before I swallowed a little and Lacy spat her share directly on my face. I couldn't believe that my mother's best friend could be such a kinky whore, but I liked that about her.

Since then, time in my house means something completely different when Jason would come over to visit Peter and Lacy to check on the house. Whenever when we have some spare time and my mom and Peter was away, a threesome always happens. But it's not always necessary for all three of us to be there. I usually have sex with Lacy when Jason and Peter were out. When Jason comes over to visit Peter, tired and bored, I like to cheer him up with a blowjob right after he enters the door. If Lacy is over, we both suck his cock. He deserves this because he is the man of the house. I know that it sounds crazy, but I my mom and brother's best friend and I hope that the awesome sex between us never stops. I know that one day it will, but until then I can enjoy Jason's cock and the tightness of Lacy's pussy, not to mention the perfect oral skills that they both possess. In our newfound experience, we know how to fuck.

AUTHOR'S NOTE

Readers: I want to expand a few of the stories to see where the characters can be explored further. If there are any of the stories that you would like to read more about again, I'd love to hear from you!

Visit my blog at http://www.ethenshear.com

Join my newsletter for free exclusive previews
http://www.ethenshear.com/in

Follow me on Twitter at
http://www.twitter.com/ethenshear

Like my page on Facebook at
http://www.facebook.com/ethenshear

Discover my books at major ebook retailers everywhere.